BAD BONES

To Jane

And with many thanks to Alix, René
and Carolina at the Royal Ground Coffee House

STRIPES PUBLISHING LIMITED
An imprint of Little Tiger Group
1 Coda Studios, 189 Munster Road,
London SW6 6AW

www.littletiger.co.uk

A paperback original
First published in Great Britain in 2015
Text copyright © Graham Marks, 2014
Extract from Flesh and Blood © Simon Cheshire, 2014
Cover copyright © Stripes Publishing Limited, 2014
Photographic images courtesy of www.shutterstock.com

ISBN: 978-1-84715-454-5

Printed and bound in the UK.

10 9 8 7 6 5 4 3

BAD BONES

GRAHAM MARKS

RED EYE

Chapter One

'Dope will get you through a time of no money better than money will get you through a time of no dope.' Gabe had read that in one of his dad's old underground, hippy comic books, he didn't remember which one. That was before his dad sold all his comics and his vinyl record collection and old-school stereo system. Before he lost his job and things started to get shitty.

That really wasn't so long ago, although it seemed like they'd been in a Time Of No Money forever. Everything had changed, and none of it for the better. Not one single damn bit.

Gabe sat on the street bench, his bike propped up next to him, watching the late-afternoon traffic go by on Ventura. Thousands of people, all with a destination, a purpose. All with money in their wallets and purses, driving on to the next stage in their sweet lives, or their neat homes, or their great jobs.

None of which applied to him, his mom, dad or little sister, Remy. They were all stuck in a house he knew for a fact was worth way less than what was owed on it, and with, so far as he could see, no chance of putting that to rights.

His mom cut coupons to save money at the supermarket like it was her religion, and everything they ate was either 'no brand', or had about ten seconds left on the 'eat by' date, or both. His dad tried to keep a brave face, but didn't always succeed, and only his sister appeared not to have a care in the world. But then Remy was nine years old. Gabe remembered being that age – when the future was always a cartoon-bright tomorrow and your life was a game. He looked down at his scuffed, frayed sneakers; it was a lot harder to think like that when you were sixteen and tomorrow did not look like it was going to be promising anything any time soon.

He stood up, stretching. He could feel the tension building in his muscles, the frustration at his total inability to figure out a way in which he could solve his family's problems; even fixing *something* would be better than doing nothing.

"Maybe…" Gabe muttered to himself, grabbing his backpack, then getting on his bike. "It'll have to be the dope."

He was about to move off when his phone chirruped: his mom's ringtone. He let the call go to voicemail, not ready to listen to whatever it was she had to say in her often tired-to-the-bone voice; it was hardly likely to be good news. No, he was not going to go home just yet, to the wired undercurrent of resentment that there was between him and his dad these days.

Gabe watched for a suitable gap in the unending stream of cars and slipped neatly into place. He had nowhere to go, but at least he might shift the dark cloud that seemed to be sitting right on top of him if he rode until it hurt. And while he rode he could think about Benny's offer.

What took him off Ventura and up towards the canyon Gabe didn't know. He'd been there before, any number of times. Generally either with friends, to get a beer buzz on, or with a girlfriend, when he had a girlfriend, for some time alone. Right now, though, with the sun beginning to set, the canyon

– empty, serene, somewhere completely elsewhere – felt like the perfect place to be.

He had hybrid Nutrak tyres on the bike, old now, though still with a few more miles left in them yet. Best of both worlds, good on and off the road, the salesman had said, back when Gabe had had spare cash to splash, and the man hadn't been bullshitting. He took to the pathway, well beaten by dog walkers and hikers, and rode into this small piece of wilderness, surrounded by the endless sprawl of LA.

He knew exactly where he wanted to be, and some ten minutes later he was up on top of a huge, smooth rock, his bike left at its graffiti-covered base. Lying down, using his backpack for a pillow, he felt the warmth the rock had soaked up during the day and was now giving off as the temperature began to drop. He was tired; tired of worrying and tired of thinking too hard about how bad things were. And they had to be bad for him to even consider working for dope-dealing Benny as an option.

Gabe closed his eyes, shutting out the world, and let the quiet chatter, hum and drone of the canyon wash over him...

He didn't know what had woken him; probably it had been the chill in the air, because he was only wearing a T-shirt and jeans. The sky, dark as it ever got in LA, had no moon yet and only a scattering of stars. Gabe sat up, scrambled around in his backpack and found his phone: 7.23. He'd slept for ages, out for the count too, as there was another missed call from his mom. It was late, so she'd no doubt be worried, and he was hungry now – hungry enough not to care about the mood round the dinner table. Time to go home.

Gabe slid down the rock, now cooler to the touch, most of its heat given back to the night, and got his bike. Standing for a moment he debated what to do, finally admitting there was no way it would be a good idea to ride out. He was going to have to walk the twisting path, which clung like ivy to the steep hillsides.

As he set off, Gabe thought about calling his mom, but decided not to. She'd only ask what he was doing, who he was with and where he was. "Well, Ma, I just woke up, alone in the canyon," wasn't what she'd want to hear. He'd figure out a better story by the time he got home.

And, kind of like the way life often is, everything went fine until it didn't.

Even when you're trying hard to be careful, if nothing goes wrong for long enough you get cocky and the lazy part of your brain stops paying as much attention as it should. That was how Gabe failed to notice how unstable the pathway was. The next step he took, the ground unexpectedly gave way, he lost his balance and, arms flailing, he fell.

It wasn't all bad. The drop turned out to be not so steep or so very far down, and also he let go of his bike and it didn't come tumbling after him. Gabe, who was fit enough and good enough to be in the school athletic team, managed the fall pretty well, skidding down the side of the narrow arroyo, arms and legs held close in. He came to a stop, slightly winded, a bit bruised but with nothing broken, in a bed of dried-up mud.

There'd been a short, sharp late-summer storm, a pretty spectacular one, the previous week. The sky had turned coal-tar black in the middle of the day, there was thunder and it seemed like a ton of water per square metre had fallen in about two minutes flat. Drains had blocked, gutters overflowed, dogs went crazy, traffic snarled up and then, as quick as it had started, it was over. All that water had had to go somewhere, and in the canyon a deluge hurtled downwards, finding any exit it could; it ripped out small trees and dislodged rocks and earth from the arroyo – brick-dry from the long, hot summer – as it raced towards the San Fernando valley.

Picking himself up, Gabe found he was in a two-maybe three-metre deep, four-metre wide cut that wouldn't have been there before the storm. As he looked around for the best way to get back up to his bike, the moon peeked over the ragged treeline behind him. Its soft, monochrome light made it seem like he was standing in an old grainy photographic negative; it gave everything a weird, spooky look.

A metre or so away from him it also picked out the distinctive shape of a human skull.

Chapter Two

It was a moment straight out of one of those CSI-type TV shows his dad loved to watch, and Gabe couldn't stop himself from going closer. He bent down, reaching out and gently brushing some dried mud off the cheekbone, as you would if someone had dirt on their face, then he pulled his hand back like he'd been burned – if this was a crime scene, a murder, he'd better not touch *anything*. He'd watched enough of those shows himself to know that.

Gabe stood up, staring at the skull; it lay kind of sideways, poking out of the earth, an empty eye socket staring sightlessly off to his right. Now he looked more carefully, he thought he could make out the shape of a shoulder bone, and further down what had to be a ribcage, next to it possibly also part of a hand. His licked his lips nervously, telling himself there was no way finding the remains of a skeleton wasn't weird.

There didn't seem to be any flesh, only bone.

So this wasn't a recent burial, more like what the cop shows called a cold case. No flesh: that made Gabe feel a lot less queasy. Then he saw a pale, yellowy glint in the moonlight. Something metallic? He knelt down and carefully scraped away a bit of earth with the tip of his finger, then some more until the curve of what could be a bracelet inset with small, light blue stones was revealed.

"Gold?" he whispered, a tight shiver crawling down his spine.

Rooted to the spot, the night air pressing in on him heavy as lead, it dawned on Gabe that the canyon, buzzing with all kinds of activity when he'd arrived, had fallen quiet. *As quiet as a grave*, said the unwanted commentator in his head.

Gabe stared into the gloom.

It was like the place was watching him, waiting to see what he did next. The silence hissed and throbbed in his ears. His chest felt like a steel belt had tightened around him, until he realized he was holding his breath. He sucked in air and shook his head. *Stupid*, he thought, *who'd be hiding out here?* And the moment that thought occurred he wished it hadn't. Any kind of crazy person *could* be here; this was LA, the place was full of them.

Gabe shivered again as the momentary hot sweat he'd broken out into cooled, his clammy T-shirt sticking to his back. He looked more carefully at what he'd found, wondering if it could really be gold. It did look kind of antique, which often meant more valuable, right? It was ethnic-looking too, and that could maybe make it worth *even* more. This was what he needed: a big, big piece of good luck!

Hands shaking slightly from excitement, he worked the earth out from around the bracelet, pushing away the thought that he was tampering with evidence as he teased it loose from a cluster of small wrist bones. Damn the law. If this could help fix things at home, even in just a small way, he had to do it.

In the palm of his hand the bracelet seemed quite small, but it weighed a lot more than he'd expected it would and looked beautiful in the moonlight. It sat there in the palm of his hand, this innocent thing he had just found, and it felt like he was watching someone else's hand. There was something about it he couldn't put into words, a feeling that this was more than just precious metal.

Kneeling there, in the chapel-like silence of the night, Gabe found himself closing his eyes and hoping more than he'd ever hoped in his life that this might be the start of things going right. A new beginning. That was what he wanted more than anything.

"Please…" he whispered, fingers gently closing round the bracelet. "*Please* be worth something, be special … *please* make a difference…"

As he spoke, Gabe felt a change in the cold metal in his hand. It was getting warmer, almost hot, like it was absorbing his body heat, and his hand tingled. He opened his eyes and looked down. The bracelet seemed to be glowing. Not simply reflecting light, but radiating it.

Gabe slowly opened his fist and frowned. As he looked at the bracelet the light faded until it was just glinting in the moonlight. He shrugged off his backpack and quickly tucked it in one of the side pockets. His mom always said he had an overactive imagination.

Picturing his mom reminded him of how late he was and he started to clamber back up to the path, then stopped. *Think straight*, he told himself. If this find *was* valuable and there was more stuff here to be dug up, he should make sure no one else stumbled on his discovery. He bent down and began trying to cover up any evidence of what he'd found.

Five minutes later, Gabe had made as good a job as he could of hiding the bones from view, and got himself back up on to the pathway. He used his house key to make a mark he figured no one else would take any notice of on a nearby tree, so he'd know exactly where to come back to. He was about to pick up his bike when he thought he heard a whisper, although maybe it was more like a sigh. He whirled round, searching for who was there, fear knotting his stomach as he prepared to run for it. Then he saw the owl.

It was perched, silent and still, on a branch near where the skeleton lay hidden. Hunched, eyes unblinking and head low, it stared back at him. *Accusingly*, Gabe thought, there was no other way to describe it.

"What?" he said, the question escaping, like a dog slipping its leash.

The owl didn't move

"Got to get out of here..." Gabe whispered, looking away as he grabbed his bike, "...else I'm gonna drive myself nuts."

He felt jittery all the way down the canyon until it finally began to level out and he could see the street that led back down to Ventura. He was about to get on his bike and start riding when the owl appeared out of nowhere. It flew over him, its huge wings outstretched, so quiet it was like someone had turned the sound right down. The bird dipped right in front of him, almost close enough to touch, then banked, turned and landed on a nearby tree. There it sat, still stooped, angry and forbidding, watching him.

Gabe had never heard of an owl attacking a person, but even so he couldn't help being spooked. The bird was making him feel guilty about what he'd done. His mom always said that a guilty conscience didn't need an accuser, as it'd do the job fine by itself. True enough, it seemed, but the bird was not helping. Gabe started riding, going as fast as he could and trying to ignore being so closely observed. Then he saw what he first took to be a couple of silver-grey dogs. They slunk out of the shadows and sat underneath the owl, staring right at him.

It took Gabe a split second to realize they weren't dogs. They were coyotes. And coyotes, unlike owls, did attack humans. He sped up, half expecting at any moment to see the animals come for him, but his last glance backwards as he made the tarmac showed neither the coyotes nor the owl had moved a centimetre.

Twenty minutes hard riding later, Gabe turned off on to his street. He'd be home in a couple of minutes. He'd got a story ready to tell his mom — that he'd been studying at his friend Anton's, with his phone still on silent from school, and had lost track of time — which should work if he didn't overdo it. And, as he'd been riding, he'd hatched a plan. He knew what to do with the bracelet he'd found. There was this place he'd seen, down towards Studio City, which sold antiques and had a sign in the window that said they did valuations. Which was exactly what he needed: a valuation.

What was this piece actually worth, if anything?

A cold breeze blew in out of somewhere, making him shiver, and on it he was sure he caught that noise again. The whisper that could be a sigh.

The owl.

Mouth instantly as dry as a packet of cheese crackers, Gabe braked and skidded to a halt, frowning as he searched the dusty orange night sky. Was his mind playing tricks on him? It must be. Had to be. And then he got that feeling, as if something was gently pressing at the back of his head, and knew he was being watched. He slowly turned and glanced over his shoulder.

The owl was right behind him.

Like a two-dimensional cardboard cut-out it was perched on a postbox that was leaning at a slightly drunken angle, away from the one next to it. The bird sat, silent and unmoving, the glint in its big round eyes the only thing that showed it was real.

The rational side of Gabe's nature tried to calm him down – why was he so freaked by a damn *owl*? It was a bird, just a bird, probably not even the one he'd seen in the canyon, right?

Wrong. It had followed him. Gabe frantically searched the shadows for any evidence the coyotes were there as well. No sign. Not yet, at least.

Get a grip. Get a grip. Get a grip… As the mantra in his head spun round and round, Gabe regained control, turned away from the owl and powered down the street, the bike's back wheel spinning to find traction.

At the gate to the side passage that led to the kitchen, he stopped to look back the way he'd come. There was nothing there. First opportunity tomorrow, straight after school, he was going to get to that place in Studio City, take whatever money he was offered for the damn bracelet and split. As he leant his bike up against the house, some way off he was sure he heard a faint hooting. Seconds later, the distant bay of a dog. Or a coyote.

He swallowed hard, telling himself not to be so stupid, but only just managed not to run for the welcoming light spilling out from the kitchen window.

Chapter Three

Gabe woke early and in a cold sweat. He felt as if he hadn't slept at all, even though his head was still full of dark, graphic dreams ... unreal, yet at the same time sharp images, which went way beyond the worst horror movies he'd ever seen. Every time he closed his eyes he could see, clear as day, right in front of him, the whole gore fest playing out in an endless loop. It was like his own personal triple-X-rated movie.

He was looking at a boy, younger than himself, who had jet black hair and olive skin. The boy was stripped to the waist and being held down, splayed out on a block of grey stone. There were six people, faces patterned with blue, red and green paint, dressed in vivid-coloured costumes, arms, necks, ears, hands all decorated with gold, their skin glistening with sweat. Two were holding the boy's arms, two his legs and one had a rope around his neck. The sixth man's face was hidden by a gold mask shaped like a skull and he was wearing an elaborate headdress with gold snakes entwined in feathers. Standing with his arms raised above the boy, in both hands the masked man held a gold knife inset with some kind of light blue stone, which gleamed in the setting sun.

The knife's arc-shaped blade slashed down into the boy's narrow, heaving chest and Gabe could hear his high-pitched scream and the crunch of shattered bone. The skull-faced figure roared as he pulled out the knife, a fountain of blood pulsing from the jagged wound, then plunged his hand into the boy's chest. The boy was still screaming when his heart was ripped out and he collapsed like a rag doll. The skull-faced priest turned towards the sun, hands held high and blood running in thick rivulets down his arms. The boy's blood was everywhere, so much it seemed impossible it could have all come from that one small body.

As the sun finally dipped below the horizon, an owl flew across the purple sky and landed beside the boy's head...

Gabe forced his eyes open and stared at the ceiling of his room, then the whole scenario, so close he could have almost reached out and touched it, blanked. The disturbingly real visions might have evaporated like mist, but they left behind a smell like someone had just lit a joint. And a malevolent sense of being watched.

Gabe sat bolt upright. He was sure he was going to find that the owl had somehow managed to get into his room during the night and was there at the end of the bed, glowering at him.

It wasn't.

In the silence his gaze wandered here and there across the untidy landscape of his room until it fell on the backpack in the corner, over by the dresser. In one of its zipped-up pockets was the object he'd found the night before. A gold bracelet, inset with light blue stone. Like the jewellery the people had been wearing in his dream. Similar, anyway. Weirdly similar.

Gabe remembered holding the bracelet in his hand, the heat of it. How it had made him feel, the way it seemed to want him to hold it tight. The thought made him shiver and he looked away.

The last thing he'd done before crashing out was to go online and try to get some information about what he'd found. The kind of stuff it would be useful to know when you're going to sell something. He'd been tired and not especially focused on what he was doing, but he had seen a couple of pieces that looked like the one he'd dug up. Aztec relics. But the

Aztecs were from Central America, so what would one of them be doing buried in a canyon in LA?

Whatever. Gabe rubbed his eyes and yawned. The only thing he could say, with any kind of certainty, was that what he'd found definitely looked like gold. It felt heavy enough to be gold. And, if he was lucky, that was what it would turn out to be. If he was lucky.

Not that he felt in any way lucky this morning. He felt beat up, dog tired and even less like going to school than he did most mornings. But what had to be done had to be done.

Gabe peeled off the damp sheet, got up, yawned so hard he thought his jaw was going to break, and then realized he had one of those low-grade headaches that cling like dirt to a bathtub. Today was going to be a trial, no doubt about that.

"You look bad. Worse than cat puke, man."

"Thanks…" Gabe squinted at Anton and frowned. For breakfast he'd had a slice of toast and half a cup of cold black coffee with an Ibuprofen chaser. He did not feel up to the witty banter and repartee that

24

was his best friend's default mode quite yet.

Anton made a pantomime act of sniffing at Gabe. "But you appear to have showered and do not *smell* like cat puke, which is good. What's the deal, bro? You got the plague or something? Or worse – maybe you are in love. You're not in *luurve,* are you? Because if you are, whoever she is, she is going to run a *mile* when she sees you. That relationship will be *over,* man…"

"Cut it out, Ant, will you?" Gabe took a deep breath and exhaled slowly. "I'm fine, just had the worst night's sleep is all. Bad dreams like you would not believe. So cut me some slack, OK?"

It was Anton's turn to frown. "Why'd you even bother coming in today, bro? You *surely* coulda swung a day off."

"I know this is gonna sound weird to you, Ant, but my house these days is *so* not a fun place that being here –" Gabe nodded down the street at the gates of Morrison High – "is my preferred option."

Anton made an 'I-am-puzzled-and-frankly-shocked' face.

"Said you were gonna think it was weird, Ant, but if I wasn't here and I wasn't at my house, what would I do? I got no money, and nowhere to go *with no money*. May as well be here, man, get the grades and learn my way out."

"You are *such* a poster boy for edja-kay-shun, Gabe."

"Like I care if I am."

This was a day that had to be got through. A series of time slots and modules – social studies/world history; math/algebra II; science/chemistry; economics; etc, etc, etc – all ticked off one after the other, at the end of which the prize was you got to go home with a bunch more work to do.

Gabe kept his head down and managed to make it from registration to release with his presence hardly being noticed. It wasn't a lot to be proud of, but there were times when a low profile was going to be the high point of the day.

He was out now, free to head over to the antique store and get himself that valuation. Wheeling his bike down the sidewalk, thankful his headache had finally gone, he sensed someone come up behind him. He turned, expecting to see Anton's crooked grin, and his heart sank.

"Benny, right? He wants a word. Like, now?"

Sean McRay, aka Scotty, Benny Gueterro's right-hand bozo, wasn't really asking, but the last thing Gabe felt like doing was having 'a word' with Benny.

"I have—"

"He's round the corner. In his … office."

Scotty, looking like Big Foot's second cousin with his long hair and beard, didn't quite put quote marks with his fingers round the word 'office', but the slight pause was enough. Because the office was a five-or-six-year-old long wheelbase Chevrolet Savana cargo van, which had an actual desk and swivel-and-tilt chair, along with a small filing cabinet, bolted to the carpeted floor in the back. Anyone else wanting a seat had to make do with foam-rubber cubes.

It was Benny's big idea. He'd seen all the TV shows where the cops raided places, and as he liked to point out: 'If you don't got a place, they can't raid it, right?' Scotty, and Nate Kansky, Benny's other right-hand bozo, both thought the big idea was not so big, but knew it was not for them to comment. Or point out that he did have a place, it was just on wheels. Right now the van was a pale grey colour, but it was resprayed on a regular basis, and also had its plates switched, part of Benny's plan to further confuse any law enforcement officers who might be paying him some unwanted attention.

Benny, himself an ex-student of Morrison High, had left before they could throw him out for his many rule infringements, not to mention sundry criminal acts. A large part of the market he catered to went to his old alma mater, but he liked to keep his distance from the place, so 'round the corner' turned out to be a couple or more blocks away. As they approached the van, the side door slid open and Scotty nodded for Gabe to go in.

"My bike…"

"I'll be here." Scotty put a meaty paw on the saddle. "It'll be here."

"You been avoiding me, Gabriel, my friend?"

For some reason Benny was just about the only person, apart from his long-dead grandma, who ever called Gabe by his full name.

"No, why would I do that?"

"I have no idea." Benny tilted back in his chair. "I make you an offer, I hear nothing."

Gabe shifted nervously on the red, nylon-covered foam cube. At any moment it felt like he was going to slide off. He leant back against the side of the van to steady himself. It was stuffy and smelled of cigarettes, dope, beer, sweat and some kind of cloying deodorant that had failed to do its job.

"I'll explain it one more time, OK?" Benny picked up a cigarette pack, opened it, shut it again and carefully put it back down on the desk. "Trying to give the damn things up… Anyway, it's like this: you need money and *I* need a little extra help around the place. A few errands running, that kind of thing. Simple. I tell you what to do, you do it and I pay you. Cash money. Like I said, simple." Benny picked up the cigarette pack again and began opening and closing the flip top. "So?"

"But—"

"But!" Benny leant forward, slamming the cigarettes on the desk. "What in hell's name is 'But'?"

"But why me, Benny? I don't get it. How'd you even know about me, know who I am?"

"Well, I do know who you are, Gabriel. And 'why you' is because *you* are not the kind of person anyone's gonna think works for *me*." Benny jabbed a finger at his chest, then sat back. "It's called misdirection, Gabriel, kinda like what magicians and suchlike do."

Gabe didn't know what to say. Misdirection? What was Benny talking about?

"It's like when people kind of *expect* to see one thing, that's what they look for and *that's* what they see," Benny went on. "People – and here when I say 'people' I mean cops, right? – well, *they* will take one look at you and think, 'nice, clean-cut type'. They will not straight-off-the-top think, 'here's a person works for Benny Gueterro'. They won't. And that's what I want."

"What if I get caught?"

"Doing what?"

"Running dope."

"Who said you were gonna be running any dope? I said 'errands'…"

30

Chapter Four

Gabe watched the van drive away down the tree-lined street, a cloud of dark brown exhaust belching out from the back. If Benny ever bothered to get the thing smog tested, which seemed highly unlikely, guaranteed it would not pass.

As the van disappeared round a corner the realization finally sank in that he was screwed. Totally screwed. There was no other way to look at it; no bright side, no 'glass half full' to this situation. Benny had made it clear as crystal that he wasn't in the mood to take no for an answer. In fact his final words had been, "Come on board, do what's asked, take the money. Or else." Had the man *really* said 'or else', like this was some playground deal? Gabe shook his head in disbelief. What he had ever done to deserve this he did not know.

"Hey…"

Gabe glanced over his shoulder. He saw a girl he'd

only recently become aware of at school… Stella, he was sure that was her name. She was standing a few metres behind him; shoulder-length dark hair, pale skin, not much make-up, wearing skinny jeans and a light blue, v-neck T-shirt. Around her neck Gabe saw she had a thin gold chain with a gold crucifix. Slung over her shoulder she had a black bag, like a camera bag, not the stuffed-to-bursting tote most of the girls hauled round with them.

He remembered thinking when he'd first seen her that she was kind of pretty but he hadn't done anything about it. Being low on funds didn't make you a 'first choice' kind of guy and he could do without being turned down flat. In fact, having seen her a few times now, he had to admit she was more than quite pretty. Kind of hot, for sure. Although right now she looked puzzled, maybe even a bit angry.

"Yeah?" Gabe assumed this Stella must be lost. "Can I help you?"

"Are you in*sane*?"

"Huh?" Gabe turned to look at the girl properly. "*What* did you say?"

"I said are you out of your mind?" The girl stood

her ground and kept eye contact. "What other reason would there be for hanging round with a moron like Benny Gueterro?"

"What's it to you who I hang with?"

"I had you down as someone with some smarts, that's all, Gabriel. Must've been wrong about that."

Gabe could not believe it. Two people in the space of fifteen minutes, both of whom called him Gabriel and thought they had him all figured out! What was he, some kind of open book?

"Now you do look sorta stupid –" Stella cracked a half grin – "with your mouth hanging open like that."

"Look… I mean, how…?" Gabe stopped, leant his bike up against a tree and took a few steps towards the girl. She didn't move. "Are you following me?"

"I don't think so, Gabriel."

"My friends call me Gabe."

"So I'm your friend now?"

"I didn't say that." Gabe couldn't work this girl out, none of the signals made any sense. "If you weren't following me, why're you here?"

"I was following Benny. You were an added extra."

Gabe looked away to give himself a moment to think, then he checked his watch to make sure he still had time to get down to Studio City.

"Oh, sorry – am I keeping you?"

"Kinda, yeah."

"Wouldn't want to do that, Gabriel…"

"What *I* don't get –" Gabe went over to his bike – "is if *I'm* mad for hanging round with Benny, what does that make *you* for following him? Possibly even taking his picture, if that's a camera bag you've got there. If you know a single thing about Benny, it would be that he is no publicity hound."

"I have my reasons."

"Yeah? Well, me too." Gabe shifted his backpack and got on the bike. "Thing is, Stella, I don't have a lot of choices right now, OK? But I'm not stupid."

"Oh, good. I'm glad about that."

Gabe shot a look at the girl; it sounded like she meant what she'd said, wasn't being ironic, but there was no way he could tell. "Yeah well, I hope you know what you're doing."

"Me?" Stella laughed, but she didn't smile. "I know *exactly* what I'm doing…"

"Man…" Anton said under his breath, shaking his head and frowning. "What the hell is going down?"

He and Gabe had been friends since forever; they were blood brothers. There were the pictures, and the scars, to prove it. Anton knew Gabe almost better than his own brother, certainly understood him a whole lot more as Milo was an off-the-curve, antisocial dweeb.

He'd had a feeling there was something up with Gabe, if his recent behaviour had been anything to go by, and in Anton's opinion it definitely was. It was also his opinion that it likely had something to do with Gabe's dad and his no-work situation, which Gabe just did not want to talk about. Up till now there hadn't ever been anything they hadn't talked about, which had made Gabe's clamming up a tad odd; what he'd just witnessed shot the whole situation up into crisis territory.

Coming out of school late, Anton had seen Gabe disappearing round a corner, walking with some tall, long-haired guy with a major beard he thought he recognized; Gabe's body language said he was not so happy about the situation so Anton made the snap decision to follow his friend. Sure, he *could* be poking his nose in where it wasn't wanted, but Gabe *might* need some backup. If nothing happened, Gabe need never know.

Staying well back, but keeping the pair in sight, Anton had just caught a glimpse of the tall dude waving Gabe into the back of some skanky old van, then staying outside with the bike. And then the penny dropped. What the hell was Gabe doing hanging with Benny Gueterro?

Anton knew all about the creep from Milo, who had attended Morrison High the same time as Benny did and had been the occasional target of his harassment. Now Benny was the go-to guy for all the stuff you were supposed to just say no to, and he was not someone you wanted to be seen with. And there was Gabe, in his freaking *van*! Could things really be that bad for his friend?

Walking past on the other side of the street, Anton made like he was deep in conversation on his cell. Some way from the van he finally managed to find somewhere he could keep watch on the situation without being seen himself. When Gabe reappeared and the van drove off, Anton had been about to call out to his friend when the girl appeared from out of nowhere. Stella Grainger. Cute girl.

She was new to Morrison, kind of an unknown quantity. Anton did a couple of the same classes as Stella, but all he had gathered was that she mostly kept herself to herself and some of the other girls thought she was kind of stuck up. So was Gabe hooking up with her? Was this something else he hadn't been talking about?

Watching out for Gabe when he could have been in trouble was a whole different ball game to watching him while he talked to a girl. That felt bad. Anton slipped away. The last thing he wanted was to be seen and have to explain to his friend why he was spying on him. Because that's what it felt like he was doing. He had to trust that Gabe would eventually tell him what was going on. It was all about trust.

Gabe rode almost on autopilot. There was so much to think about, so many things happening all at once. Why did life have to be so damn complicated? He felt as if everything was beginning to spiral out of control. It had been hard enough to juggle the home and school situations without Benny walking in and acting like he had the right to make demands. Although, if the man was telling the truth and all he really wanted was an errand boy, then the money might help ease the pressure at home. And if the gold bracelet he'd found was worth something, and there was more like it to be dug up, that would be even better. But the overriding feeling he had was that at any moment he was about to fumble and drop something.

To top it all he now had this girl, Stella, sticking her nose in where it really wasn't wanted. Why did people assume they could do that? He thought about Stella for a moment, about how sure of herself she'd been, like she knew so much more than he did. He briefly wondered what *her* story was.

But he had way too much on his plate already for that kind of stuff right now, including the whole owl and coyote thing. Thinking that he had animals following him didn't help matters much, either. It was weird, but the dreams had been *way* weirder. Did it all mean anything? Who the hell knew, certainly not him. Unlike Stella, he wasn't sure of anything.

Gabe dropped a gear and sped up. He just hoped whoever owned the antique store didn't give him the runaround.

Chapter Five

The store looked closed – lights on, but no one home – although the sign on the door clearly stated that its opening hours were 10.30am to 6pm, and it was only 5.05. Gabe looked back at his bike, chained to a bench, just checking again that he'd done what he already knew for sure he had, then pressed the entry buzzer. Nothing happened. He was about to press the button again when there was a loud *click*, which meant some unseen person was letting him in. Pushing the door open, Gabe glanced up and saw a small CCTV camera staring back at him. He obviously did not look dangerous.

As the door swung to and locked behind him, he noticed there were at least two more cameras pointing his way, and for a second he wondered if he was now trapped, unable to get out unless he was let out. He stood in the shop, unsure of what to do next, and waited, listening to clocks ticking out of synch with each other.

The place didn't appear to specialize in anything particular; there was silverware on show, pieces of overly ornate furniture, items of jewellery and some paintings in heavy gilt frames. Gabe didn't know if the stuff was seriously valuable, but on the other hand it didn't feel like he was standing in a thrift store surrounded by junk.

"Can I help you, young man?"

Gabe jerked round and saw a man had come out from the back of the shop and was standing behind a glass-topped counter. He was tall, perma-tanned and turning jowly, his thinning, very black hair cut short and spiky. He was wearing a dark suit and a strawberry pink shirt, with shot cuffs but no tie. It was a look, but Gabe hadn't a clue what it was trying to achieve.

"I saw your sign…"

"Good," the man cleared his throat and looked at his polished fingernails. "That was its purpose."

"The one saying you did valuations?"

"Ah, *that* sign."

"And I have something…" Gabe swung off his backpack, careful not to knock anything over – this

41

was definitely a 'You break it, you buy it' place – and knelt down to unzip one of the pockets.

"Is this a family heirloom? Does it belong to you?" The man raised his eyebrows, head slightly on one side.

"No… I mean, yes…" Gabe stood up, unfolding the old duster he'd wrapped round the bracelet and kicking himself for not thinking he might be asked where he'd got it from. "It isn't a family thing, but, yeah … you know … it, um, it belongs to me."

"May I?" The man beckoned Gabe over to the counter.

Gabe didn't move. Actually, he couldn't move and he had no idea why. He was here in this shop for one reason only: to find out how much the bracelet was worth. And to do that he had to let this man see it…

"Do you want a valuation, or not?"

Gabe looked at the man, feeling the tension building in his shoulders. He nodded. "Yes … yes, I do…"

"Well –" the man sniffed and gave a swift, humourless smile – "I don't have all day."

"Sure…" Gabe pushed away the urge to leave and held out his hand, feeling a strange sensation of betrayal as he did so.

The man took the bracelet from him in a way that made it appear as if he wasn't at all sure whether it was clean or not. He then switched on a lamp and got a small jeweller's magnifying glass out of a drawer. "Now, let me see…"

Gabe watched the man get the feel of the weight in his hand and saw his eyebrows do the little jump that happens when you prove yourself wrong. The man had thought he was being given a piece of cheap garbage, and now he was thinking otherwise. Gabe became aware that he was breathing in an almost panicky way, that he didn't like watching someone else with the bracelet. *His* bracelet… He shook his head and tried to overcome the feeling, but it wouldn't let go.

The man bent forward, eyeglass jammed to his face, closely examining the bracelet from every possible angle. It seemed to take forever but finally he put it down on the counter top. "Excuse me *just* one second…"

"Sure, OK."

Gabe watched the man disappear into the back of the shop and quickly picked up the bracelet, an unexpected sense of relief flooding through him as he closed his fingers round it. He'd got the distinct impression the man was if not excited then extremely interested, and he wondered what would happen next. What would he do if the man wanted to buy it right there and then?

Instead of trying to figure out the answer to that question, he looked down at the velvet-lined trays under the glass. One had a display of old watches, hands all set to exactly ten minutes past ten, another displayed ranks of sparkling diamond rings, and a third contained various lockets and chains. Everything here had been brand new once, each piece probably somebody's prized possession; he wondered about the different paths they'd taken to all end up here, in a cabinet, at the back of some shop in Studio City. The slight cough of someone clearing their throat made Gabe look up. The man was back.

"It's nice… It's, ah, very nice, in its way. I just, ah –" the man gestured towards the rear of the shop, smiling and nodding – "I just checked and I'd say it was worth, oh, I don't know, maybe a hundred, hundred and fifty bucks. Or so? Around that."

Gabe was shocked; the man was treating him like a kid and hadn't even bothered to *try* and lie like he meant it.

"Oh, and yes … I was wondering…" the man frowned, looking down at the spot on the counter where he'd left the bracelet. "You have it?"

Gabe nodded.

"Yes, well, as I say, I was wondering whether there was … whether you had anything else like this? By any chance?"

"No." Gabe slowly moved the hand holding the bracelet behind his back. "No, I don't. And thanks for the 'valuation'. I'll think about it."

"Look, I'm sorry if you didn't like the price – why don't you let me take another look? Maybe I can do better…"

"I have to go." Gabe put the bracelet in his pocket. "But thanks anyway."

"Look, this is, how shall I say, a *bargaining* situation. It's what we do in the antiques business! It's a trade, like in a souk, if you know what I mean? I say a price, you say a price, we dance a little?" The man actually performed some weird little dance movement. "And then, what we end up doing, we come to an agreement everyone's happy with. That is what we do – how we do business…"

"Well, I don't have the time to do that today, mister—"

"LeBarron, Mr LeBarron," the man interrupted, reaching into his breast pocket and bringing out a business card, which he offered to Gabe. "Call me if you change your mind."

Chapter Six

Outside the shop, Gabe stood on the sidewalk looking at the card. *LeBarron Antiques and Collectibles*, it said, in two lines of flowery script that you could feel when you ran your finger over it, underneath which was the name Cecil LeBarron, in a plain font, and right at the bottom, in that same font but smaller, the address, phone number and website.

Gabe stuffed the card in his back pocket and went over to the bike. He was totally sure the bracelet was worth more than a hundred and fifty dollars. Way, *way* more. Had to be, or why had Mr Cecil LeBarron acted like he did? So the first thing he had to do was go straight back to the canyon and find out if there was any more to be dug up before anyone else came along and discovered the skeleton. Second thing: do some proper research.

He'd dialled in the four-digit code for the bike lock, and was wrapping the bracelet in the duster when the unsettling sensation of being watched crawled over him again. The same feeling he'd had when he woke up that morning, only much stronger this time. Then his right hand locked solid round the bracelet. Freaked by what was happening, Gabe's head swivelled like he was at a pro-tournament tennis match, searching for any sign of an owl, or even a coyote.

Not a thing.

Gabe stared down at his hand, the bracelet held in its claw-like grip. His arm hurt bad, and the intense pain was creeping up towards his shoulder. Panic was starting to take hold of him again when something made him stop and slowly look up. On a bench right opposite him sat a man. Just some old guy wearing a tatty yellowy-brown leather jacket, dusty work boots and washed-out jeans, so pale they were almost white above the knees. A faded red baseball cap was pulled low enough to make it impossible to see the man's eyes, but Gabe knew he was staring straight at him. And he knew he'd seen him before.

Last night. The man had been in his dreams last night...

Gabe's stomach did a flip, and he dragged his gaze away from the man. He felt like he'd been punched in the gut. Images from the horrific dreams came flooding back, only now they looked like a shaky, badly made film playing in his head, complete with a hissed and whispered soundtrack that was impossible to understand. This person across the street wasn't dressed like the masked figure had been, and he wasn't wielding a blood-spattered gold knife or wearing a feathered headdress.

But the man across the street had been right there, killing the boy.

Sometimes in dreams you just knew things without actually seeing them.

Right now, in broad daylight, Gabe knew that this person, his face half obscured, was the same man he'd seen pull the living, beating heart out of the boy on the altar. There was no doubt. Gabe could feel the cold, fanatical anger radiating from him.

A breeze blew past, bringing with it the sharp, pricking aroma of burnt herbs. The smell funnelled straight up his nostrils and into his brain, intensifying the sounds and the pictures, for a moment making what was going on in his head more real than the world around him.

Fighting back, Gabe clutched at the only thought that made any kind of sense. He had to get away – *now*.

The sudden rush of adrenaline coursing through his bloodstream jolted Gabe into action, shaking off whatever had been paralyzing him. Stashing the bracelet and lock he grabbed his bike and launched off the sidewalk and on to the road without looking. Behind him he heard the screech of tyres and a horn blaring, but he didn't care. He just had to put some distance between himself and the person across the street.

Someone he'd never seen before, except in his dream.

Which was not only crazy, it was impossible.

Wasn't it?

Gabe rode, hunkered down and pedalling manically, flying through a couple of traffic lights *way* after he should have stopped, weaving between cars and getting in and out of spaces the sane part of him knew were much too close for comfort. But for a mile or more the sane part of him hadn't been in control, not until the adrenaline had worn off and he could finally allow himself to coast to a halt. Panting like a beast, for a moment he had no idea where he was.

Covered in sweat, lungs heaving and muscles screaming, Gabe slowly calmed down. It was only when his heartbeat had settled back to something approaching normal that he saw his 'escape route' had brought him within easy striking distance of the canyon. It was where he'd been planning to come, before he'd gotten totally spooked by losing control of his hand, then seeing the man across the street. But now ... now he wasn't so sure he wanted to go back up there, even in broad daylight.

Before he'd freaked out seeing the man sitting opposite LeBarron Antiques and Collectables, his main doubts about returning to the canyon had been being found by a Park Ranger. He realized what he'd done the night before was wrong. Not real *bad* wrong, like murder or whatever, but not right, either, and no doubt illegal. He wasn't stupid, he knew the difference between right and wrong, but that wasn't what was getting to him.

For the most part the Law seemed to be all about whether you either got caught or you didn't.

Like school, but on a whole different level in terms of punishment. Last night, as he fell asleep, the way Gabe thought about it was that what he'd done couldn't hurt anyone, and as it could really help his family it was, therefore, no biggie. He was beginning to have second thoughts because of the gold bracelet nestling oh so innocently in his backpack.

Life now was either 'Before Bracelet' or 'After Bracelet'. Before Bracelet, all he'd ever associated skeletons with had been the 'woo-hoo-spooky!' cartoon nonsense at Halloween. Before Bracelet he'd never had a real nightmare in his entire life, certainly never been followed by a damn owl. After Bracelet he'd turned into this superstitious idiot, making connections where there were none. Was he simply giving coincidences a meaning they just didn't have?

"Owls are nocturnal, right?" he muttered to himself, even as he checked the sky and the deep shadows between buildings. "They're fricking *nocturnal*, dammit."

Twenty minutes later, Gabe stood in the parking area by the entrance to the canyon, giving himself a final talking to. Like what was there to worry about anyway? Nada. The man across the street was just some guy who, coincidentally, happened to look *somewhat* like a person he'd had a crappy dream about. So what? And the thing with his hand was just like a muscle spasm, a cramp. Nothing more.

So, if he didn't go and see what else there was to dig up, all he'd have was something he was pretty damn sure was worth a whole lot more than a hundred and fifty bucks. And that would be it.

He didn't have a choice. If he was going to have any chance of helping his family he *had* to go back to what he couldn't stop himself from thinking of as 'the burial site'. Except it wasn't a body, not really. It was some old bones. That was all. Just a load of bones.

Chapter Seven

It turned out the canyon was virtually empty; he'd so far seen a solitary dog walker some way away, and that was it. Plus it all looked so different in the bright sunlight. Even after what had happened yesterday, he would have to be a complete wimp to be scared by rocks and trees and brush. He was being extra-vigilant and wary because he did not want to get caught by a Park Ranger. That was all.

The fact that nothing, completely nothing, had occurred the whole way up to the tree Gabe had marked the night before was almost worse than if something had. It felt like a total comedown; all that worry, for what? Once he'd found a place that was as out of sight as possible to stash his bike, he got down to business. He wouldn't be long. He'd be able to see exactly what he was doing and this time he wouldn't have to bother trying to cover his tracks. In-N-Out, like the burger chain.

Gabe had come prepared for the job, having taken a small gardening trowel and a small paintbrush from the workbench at the back of the garage before he left for school. Getting them out of his backpack, he set to work.

As he dug, Gabe could feel himself becoming more and more agitated and twitchy. Much more nervous than he should have been if getting caught was all he was worried about. But he stayed, drawn to the promises he'd seen in the yellow glow of the gold bracelet.

Half an hour later he'd unearthed a tiny medallion, followed by three heavy, jewelled rings. And then he found something that scared the hell out of him. A gold knife, inset with light blue stones, with an arc-shaped blade. Exactly like the one he'd seen in his awful dream.

Gabe sat back on his heels and stared at the knife, searching for any signs of blood, mesmerized by the fact that he was holding something he'd dreamed about. Something he'd seen kill a boy. He was kind of shocked by how it felt, holding it. Having this knife, owning it, made him … he couldn't quite put into words how it made him feel. Strong, maybe even untouchable. And he wanted to keep it. Forever. He finally made himself put the knife down and checked his cell. Time to get back to digging. That was what he was here for – he could sit and look at what he'd found back home.

Some five minutes later, he finished teasing the dirt away from a nine- maybe ten-centimetre high crucifix. He carefully pulled it out, cleaned off the earth and turned it over. It was heavy, a solid chunk of precious metal, and it was different from everything else he'd found. The medallion, the rings and the bracelet were in pretty good condition, as was the knife, but the cross was twisted badly out of shape and the figure of Christ was all battered. And it looked warped, like it might have been in a fire.

Gabe glanced at the rest of his haul and then back at the crucifix, wondering what this obviously Christian object was doing with a bunch of stuff that was so definitely *not* Christian. Especially the knife. The only word to describe the knife was pagan. Finding the two things together didn't make sense

The crucifix, like the knife, also had an almost visible power to it, making him feel as if it needed to be protected, kept safe. It wanted to be held.

Gabe shivered. He needed time to take everything in, deal with the wildly conflicting reactions in his head and his gut. A cautious voice was telling him to put the stuff back, insisting that no good would come of having it. But a raw, more feral instinct reacted vehemently to the very idea of leaving the gold behind. And it was winning the argument.

Gabe turned his attention back to the skeleton. This body, this person, had to have been buried out here in the middle of nowhere, who knew how long ago, for a good reason. And the only one he could think of was that the people who had done it hadn't wanted him ever to be found. This was a person who was supposed to have disappeared. Gabe shivered again, noticing for the first time how the skeleton's jaw was wide open, like the person was silently screaming as they drowned in the earth … as if they had been buried alive.

Unbidden, his imagination began to put layers of flesh back on to the bones, building up an all-too-real picture of what this person might once have looked like. He pushed the image away, an irrational fear of unintended consequences gripping him. If he wasn't careful, might these remains come back to life?

Sometimes he hated his brain.

"Who the hell were you, anyway?" he muttered, frowning as he stood up. "And what are you doing here?"

They were both good questions, and he was surprised they hadn't occurred to him before. If there were stories behind how all those things for sale in Cecil LeBarron's place had ended up there, then there *had* to be a doozy of a one about how this particular body, and everything he'd so far found with it, had come to be here in the canyon. A place that was way off the beaten track now, so must've been even more remote back when the body was buried.

This couldn't be the grave of someone anybody had cared much for — it wasn't six feet under in a cemetery and there was no sign of a coffin, for starters. And something was off about this whole thing; he couldn't ignore the way he was feeling. He looked at the cross again and couldn't shake the idea that the damage had been done on purpose. He wasn't religious, but for some reason it made him feel kind of bad. What had happened to it?

Gabe checked his phone again, surprised to see

how long he'd been so focused on the job; the time had run away and he'd forgotten where he was, forgotten to worry about being found. He should go.

But there was more to do.

It was late, though, and he could easily spend at least another hour digging and still not even have got to half of the skeleton.

But there was more to do!

A feeling of intense rage flooded over him. Why was he so angry at himself? Something was wrong. He really should go. Go now. Wrapping the new finds in the duster, along with the original bracelet, Gabe wondered how much all seven pieces would be worth.

Again a blast of anger hit him. These things were special! The knife wasn't just antique, it was ancient! And, like the crucifix, it was sacred – he knew that, he had seen the knife being used. He'd held it in his own hands. How could he think of these things in terms of money? How could he?

Now he wasn't so totally focused on digging things up, Gabe was more aware of his surroundings. Once again on high alert, he stayed still and quiet, closing his eyes and listening for the whisper of wings or the near-silent pad of coyote paws. But there was nothing to hear.

And then there was.

Something ... *in his head.*

A murmur of voices, or maybe just one single voice – he couldn't be sure. The sound echoed, bringing memories of his nightmare back into sharp focus. The sound of the voice rooted Gabe to the spot. It was bad enough recalling dark, blood-soaked dreams, but so much worse to be pulled back into them in broad daylight. Then a high-pitched whine set up, rising to a screech that felt as if it was trying to cut straight through his brain. Gabe clapped his hands to his ears in a vain attempt to shut out the noise.

A feeling of cold dread took over and blanked out everything else. Fear made him want to run, just abandon ship and take the quickest route out of the arroyo, but he had enough self-control left to start scrambling back up to get his bike instead.

Grabbing at anything to help him get up the slope, Gabe was shocked to see his fingers were bleeding when he got to the top. It took a moment before he realized there were no cuts anywhere on his hands, that the blood was just smeared. He slowly raised his hands to his ears and touched them, fingers coming away daubed with red. His *ears* were bleeding? Gabe stood on the pathway, shaking and staring at his hands, unable to take in what had happened, half believing he was seeing things, dimly aware that the screeching in his head had stopped.

Chapter Eight

Gabe pulled off his backpack, tore open one of the zipped compartments and pulled out the roughly knotted cloth. He stood, weighing the gold trove in his hand. Long seconds ticked by, time seeming to stretch.

Choices.

He hated choices, always sure he was bound to make the wrong one.

But here and now it was so simple: keep the gold, or forget he'd ever found the damned stuff.

Because he couldn't ignore the obvious truth that there was more, *so* much more, to these things he'd dug up than what they appeared to be on the surface. It was so … the only word he could think of was *possessive*, but that was ridiculous. People possessed objects, not the other way round. Didn't they? He hated himself for even thinking this could be otherwise, didn't want to act like some kind of stupid, scared kid who believed in ghosts and ghouls and all that fairy-tale shit. But he couldn't help it. His *ears* were bleeding ferchrissake!

Gabe stared down at the bundle. He so wanted to throw it back down the arroyo, yet also desperately needed to keep the gold. The confusion was dizzying. Throw away or keep… Keep or sell and get the money? He could feel himself being ripped apart by the conflict battling it out inside him. The pressure inside his skull had reached migraine levels, the muscles in his arm were stretched to breaking point, vibrating with the strain of waiting to be told what to do, waiting to see which side in this messed-up duel finally won the day.

And it was a close-run thing.

The primal forces, fear of the unknown and superstition put up a fierce struggle against the voices of reason and logic. Not to mention what his old Grandad Mike had used to call dollars and sense. 'When money talks, even if it's in a whisper,' he'd say, tapping the table top with a nicotine-stained finger, 'you'll find folks have a tendency to listen.' He had been referring to politicians, whom he'd generally disliked and distrusted, whichever party they belonged to, but that thought had, in the end, swayed Gabe and made him return the gold to the sanctuary of his backpack. Dollars and sense...

Gabe dusted himself down and hoped he'd managed to get rid of the worst of the blood – tough to do with spit, an already-grubby tissue and no mirror. If he was lucky and managed to sneak unseen into the house he could finish the job off when he got home. At least he hoped that was the way it was going to go, because he hadn't been able to come up with a single decent idea to explain away bloody ears to his mom.

Unsurprisingly, the headache had come back. He'd tried to be Zen and pedal in time to its dull, insistent throb, but that hadn't made it any easier to figure out what to do. He knew it'd be better if the gold wasn't in the house. The only other place he could keep it that was even remotely safe was his locker at school. Hardly high security, but he couldn't think of anywhere else.

The first thing he should do was at least try and find out the value of what he'd got his hands on.

And then there was the question of whether he went back to Mr Cecil LeBarron's Studio City store or looked for somewhere else.

As he turned into his street he thought that Mr LeBarron might be the best bet to start with. The man was interested, and knew he'd screwed up today, which Gabe figured kind of gave him the upper hand. If he hadn't driven himself crazy before he could get there.

"Hey, Gabe…"

Anton? Gabe wobbled and nearly fell off his bike, jolted out of his thoughts by his name being called.

"You OK, man?"

Gabe braked to a halt and looked behind him. Anton was walking to meet him. "Yeah, fine… I'm fine. You? What're you doing here?"

"Kinda waiting for you." Anton shrugged, his smile lopsided. "Missed you at the end of school, wanted to check how your day was, you know? You being so kind of out there this morning."

This morning.

So much had happened since then… Benny, Stella, Cecil LeBarron, the weirdness up in the canyon. "No, I'm good, Ant, really…"

"We go back a long way, right?" Anton didn't sound so sure of himself.

"Yeah, we do. Long way."

"We always talk about stuff, right? Like we always *have* talked about stuff…" Anton didn't seem to know whether to stay where he was or move closer to Gabe. "Anyway, look, I just wanted to say, you want to talk you can, you know, talk … to me. Right?"

"I know." A feeling of extreme tiredness washed over Gabe. He knew he should talk to Ant, about everything. About how hard it was to deal with his dad being out of work, about being held over a barrel by Benny Gueterro and having Stella on his case. And the skeleton and the gold. Maybe, after a decent night's sleep, he'd feel up to it, but not now.

"Gabe?"

"Sorry, Ant." Gabe found it hard to look his friend straight in the face. "Really … I gotta get home right now, but I'll call you. I will."

"Make sure you do." Anton waved, looking over his shoulder as he walked away. "Blood brothers, Gabe, don't forget that."

Gabe watched his friend turn the corner at the

end of the street; Anton didn't look back and for a moment Gabe wondered why that made him feel a bit sad, then the reality of his situation pushed the thought away.

He was about to ride off when his phone rang, not one of his designated ring tones. He looked at the number, which he didn't recognize, except that it was local. Ant had recently been chewing his ear off about how he was getting an upgrade and changing services, and it would be just like him to call when he was only round the corner. On the off-chance it was Ant, Gabe picked up the call; the least he could do was apologize for the way he'd just been.

"Hi, Ant, that you?"

"Gabriel…"

"Stella? How the—?"

"Never mind how. You should forget Benny, you really should."

Gabe took the phone away from his ear and stared at it for a second, like that would help him make more sense of what was going on. "What?"

"Like I told you, Gabriel, don't have anything to do with that lowlife creep."

"So, OK … like what makes you think you … like, why d'you think you can tell anyone what to do?"

Stella laughed, the reception so clear, her voice sounding as if she was standing right by him; Gabe couldn't stop himself from looking. No sign.

"Just don't do it. He's stupid and he's trouble."

"Look—"

The call was cut and Gabe found himself listening to the sound of silence. He stared at the screen again, angry and confused. What right did this girl have to tell him how to run his life? Even if he couldn't fault her on her character analysis of Benny, which was entirely spot on. And somehow that made him even madder, being second-guessed and outmanoeuvred by someone he hardly knew, who hardly knew him. He almost punched 'call back' so he could demand to know why she cared what he did. Instead he jammed the phone in his back pocket and rode off. He did not have the energy.

The car wasn't parked outside when Gabe got home and he walked down the passage towards the kitchen, mentally crossing his fingers that he might get some time in the house on his own. It didn't work. His dad was there at the table drinking a coffee, reading the paper. The funnies, not the Jobs Vacant pages, either. Typical.

The timing was less than perfect. On top of really needing to get himself cleaned up properly, for the last few weeks it had taken a major effort on Gabe's part to have anything even approaching a civil conversation with his dad. His mom had called him out on his behaviour, told him he was being unreasonable. She said he had no idea how hard it was for someone who wanted to work not to be able to get a job. Gabe had wanted to say did she have *any* idea how hard it was to have a dad who didn't look like he was trying very hard to get a job, but managed not to. That would have done nothing except hurt his mom.

"Anton came by earlier, looking for you." Gabe's dad put down the paper and sat back in his chair. "He find you?"

"Yeah, he did."

"Good."

"Yeah..." Gabe made for the door.

"Everything OK with you?"

"Sure." Only a couple of steps to go, nearly there.

His dad sighed and shook his head, a pained expression on his face. "You know the one thing we've *never* done in this family?"

There was no way Gabe could get away with not answering. "No, what?"

Vern looked his son straight in the eye. "We never lied to each other, is what."

Gabe felt like he'd been caught between a rock and a hard place. His dad was right, he was lying, everything was not OK; but whose fault was that? He knew that if he let rip now it would be bad and he would regret it later, but why should he always be the one cutting slack and being understanding? Who was the grown-up here?

"I can't make you talk to me, Gabe." His dad stood up, pushing the chair back, and walked past his son. "But I'll be here, when you want to," he said as he left the room. "If you want to."

Gabe stood in the empty, silent kitchen. With nothing to focus on, no target, his pent-up anger left a sour, metallic taste in his mouth. When life sucked it was a bitch, and it sure as hell sucked now.

Chapter Nine

This time the dreams were so much worse. Hyper-real, beyond hi-def, with every sense magnified to unimaginable extremes.

The colours of the costumes were even more clashing and vivid, the woven patterns more jagged. The sounds were needle-sharp and they hurt, the atmosphere so heavy and cloying he felt as if he was running out of air to breathe.

And this time he could smell the fear radiating off the victim, another young boy, as he was led right past him. Watching him being picked up and placed on the altar, Gabe retched at the thought of all the blood spilled on it by the thousands of souls who had died there. He looked down and saw the stones used to build the pyramid had been stained a dark, dark black by the gore that had soaked into them. So much blood no amount of rain could ever wash it away.

Light from the setting sun flashed off the golden knife – the exact same knife he now had in his possession – and drew his attention to the man holding it. It occurred to Gabe that maybe he was some kind of priest, although the guttural noises he was making, along with the elaborate feathered headdress, made him look and sound more like a crazed bird. Then he noticed the crucifix. This man also had a crucifix, like the one he'd found, except not all bent and damaged.

There was something odd about the cross, but before he had a chance to think about what it was the priest let out a roar and Gabe knew what was going to happen. Death was being called upon. This truly hateful scene was pulling Gabe in with its terrible, graceful savagery. And what made it so much worse was that he could see some kind of awesome, insane beauty about what was happening in front of him.

That was when Gabe woke up, covered in sweat. The room was pitch black and for a second he panicked that he'd gone blind. Then the soft, fluorescent green glow from the display of his alarm clock pushed away the dark just a little and he saw it was 3.34am. Now 3.35am…

Gabe lay flat on his back, exhausted. His skin crawled like he was covered in ants and he felt as if he'd been to … the word 'hell' squirmed and skittered around in the back of his mind waiting to be let out and he tried as hard as he could to ignore it. Hell was other people. Someone famous had said that, and he wanted to believe it was true and that was all it was. He did not want to believe it was crazed, knife-wielding people and lost souls, blood-soaked altars and sacrifices to unknown gods.

The thought of going back to sleep was laughable.

More of what he'd just been through? No way.

Gabe dragged himself out of bed and padded down to the bathroom, the corridor lit by the plug-in night lamp his sister still said she needed. He closed the door and switched the light on. In the mirror over the sink an exhausted, freaked-out version of himself stared back. He looked like shit. Running the cold tap he sluiced his face and rinsed his mouth out; it was only when he saw the blood running away that he realized he must have bitten the inside of his lip. He checked his ears to see if they'd repeated their performance from earlier in the canyon. They hadn't. He dried off and sat on the toilet lid, elbows on his knees and hands cradling his head. He felt lousy. His life genuinely was crap, whichever way you looked at it, and now he couldn't even escape from what was going on with a good night's sleep.

He sighed heavily. Tomorrow was another day. And tomorrow he and his family would still be facing the same problems. Tomorrow he had to work for Benny, and who knew what that might entail. Tomorrow he would also have to try and get rid of at least some of the damn gold. Although looking on the bright side, if that was at all possible, if Benny and Mr Cecil LeBarron both paid up, the day *after* tomorrow might feasibly be better.

Yeah, right.

"Gabey-Gabey-Gay-ay-ay-bee, hugging his pillow like a bay-ay-ay-bee!"

Gabe jerked awake to see his sister, Remy, bending over and peering at him like he was some weird zoo exhibit.

"Scram, Remy," he muttered, turning over and squinting at the clock; he found it hard to believe he'd actually fallen back to sleep, not had any nightmares he could remember and that it was now 7.06am… make that 7.07.

"What've you got there, Gabey?" Remy pointed at his bedside table, reaching forward like she was going to touch the untidily knotted cloth duster.

"Nothing, now move it!"

"Well, Mom says you'd better get your skates on, else you'll be late for school…" Remy dodged the dirty sock Gabe launched at her as she made for the door. "And you got dribble on your chinny-chin-chin…"

"Get…"

Remy disappeared, then her head popped round the door, excited. "Guess what I saw in the front yard this morning, Gabey."

"A fight between two of your stupid dolls?" Remy crossed her eyes and did her 'you're so dumb' face, which always cracked Gabe up. "OK, OK, I give up, what?"

"An owl, Gabey. Just sitting there on the mailbox, kinda *looking* at the house."

Ten minutes later, showered and shaved, Gabe still felt jumpy and nervous, as if any minute something dreadful was going to happen. The owl was watching. Not *an* owl, but *the* owl. Had to be. He didn't feel hungry any more.

As he went into the kitchen Remy was leaving, giving him a saccharine-sweet smile that ended with her sticking out her tongue; Gabe ignored her, which he knew drove her crazy, but that was only fair as it was all she ever did to him. He saw his mom over by the dishwasher, unloading it with the morning newscast on KZLA, a local TV channel, on in the background. No sign of his dad. They hadn't said much to each other since yesterday, and he was kind of glad he wasn't around now. The less stress the better, the way he was feeling.

"Hi, Gabe, sleep well, sweetheart?"

"Yeah, OK, Mom." Gabe thought about what his dad had said, about how they didn't – and by implication, shouldn't – lie to each other in this family; well, if not telling his mom about the kind of dreams he'd had last night was lying, so be it. He glanced at the TV, showing a reporter, station-branded microphone in his hand, looking earnestly at the camera. "What's the big story?"

"Someone's gone missing, I think they said over by Daisy Canyon. They showed a picture. Older person, a guy wearing a red baseball cap. I wasn't paying too much attention. Must be a slow news day."

Gabe was glad his mom wasn't looking at him as he felt the colour drain from his face. *Way* too many coincidences for comfort.

"Before you ask if there's any chance of some French toast this morning, we're out of eggs, sweetie, sorry –" his mom carried on talking with her back to him – "I could nuke a slice of pizza?"

"OK, thanks…" Pizza for breakfast. Oh joy. Never the ideal choice, but he had a hard day ahead of him and knew he should eat something.

"Want a glass of milk with that?"

"Yeah, that'd be great." Gabe went over to the table, knowing that to refuse food would be like sending up a warning flare: Something Is Wrong With My Son! "Could you do me a favour, Mom? Could you tell Remy, *again*, that she's not allowed to even step inside my room? I don't go in hers, right?"

"Sure, but I don't know what the problem is." Gabe's mom put a glass of milk on the table as the microwave pinged. "What's she going to do, steal your dirty laundry? She'd be doing you a favour if she did."

"She just gets in my face." Gabe accepted the plate his mom gave him, the cheese on the pizza slice bubbling like yellow lava; breakfast appeared to be an ogre's severed tongue.

"Give it a few years, when she and her little friends aren't so little any more…"

Gabe turned to see his dad, whom he hadn't heard coming into the kitchen; he hadn't shaved.

Glancing at the kitchen clock, which was always a little slow, Gabe leapt up from the table. "Geez, look at the time – I gotta go!"

Snatching up the pizza slice, he hared back down the corridor, past his sister going the other way, and skidded into his room. He flung everything he needed for school in his backpack and was halfway back to the kitchen when he remembered the gold, wrapped up in the raggedy old duster and waiting on his bedside table. Swearing at himself under his breath for his abject stupidity, he ran back to his room and got it.

Disaster averted, goodbyes yelled and his head in a whirl, he exited the kitchen and grabbed his bike. Then he stopped and thought about what his mom had said. If he'd got to the kitchen a little earlier he would have seen the picture, known if the man she'd described was the same person he'd seen. Now all he could do was torment himself, something he seemed to have a talent for. He went to the side door, pulling it open very slowly.

No owl on the mailbox.

Could Remy have made it all up?

Chapter Ten

Gabe was finished, and now a hundred and fifty dollars better off for his troubles, which, to be honest, hadn't been so bad. He had no idea what was in the envelopes Benny had given him, but the people he'd delivered them to had seemed happy enough to get them. And the places he'd been sent to turned out to be just normal offices, one place was quite a high-end shoe shop, not the scuzzy backstreet dives he'd imagined he'd be going to.

Tucked away in his wallet were two crisp fifties and two slightly less crisp twenties and a couple of crumpled fives. *More where that came from*, Benny had said, also saying he'd need Gabe again in a couple of days. Gabe checked his phone, surprised to see it was just after five in the afternoon and he still had plenty of time to get over to Studio City before Mr Cecil LeBarron closed up shop for the night. He had the original bracelet with him – the rest of the find was in his locker – and if he could sell it for a reasonable price today that would be a result.

As far as he could tell he hadn't been followed – by cops, owls or coyotes – and if this had been some TV detective show he was in it would easily have won the gold statuette for Most Boring Script. But Gabe still couldn't get rid of the oppressive feeling that he was being watched. It was with him the whole time, like a stink that wouldn't wash off, and he didn't know if it was doing the job for Benny or the gold bracelet in his backpack that was the cause. Maybe, he thought, it was both.

Getting back on his bike he set off for the antique store.

"I wasn't at all sure I'd see you again." Cecil LeBarron held back the door to let Gabe in. Today he was wearing a red and white pinstripe shirt, a dark blue jacket with gold buttons and some kind of coat of arms on the breast pocket and jeans with a razor-sharp crease. Another look Gabe could not decode.

"Me, either."

81

"What made you change your mind, if I might ask?" Cecil LeBarron gestured for Gabe to follow him to the back of the store.

"You said you wanted to have another look, maybe make a different offer, right?" Cecil nodded, a slightly confused look working its way across his salon-tanned features. "So I came back."

"Better the devil you know, in a manner of speaking." Cecil went behind the glass-topped counter and held out a hand that was the total opposite of Benny's, each nail beautifully manicured and polished, not a nicotine stain in sight. "May I?"

Gabe started to get the bracelet out of his backpack; all he wanted to do was be rid of the thing. Except now the moment had arrived, that was not how it was panning out. With the bracelet in his hand, warm to the touch, he felt an overpowering bond. He and it belonged together. He did not want to hand it over. He couldn't hand it over.

"May I?" Cecil repeated, one eyebrow raised. "Please?"

Gabe looked at the man in front of him. Part of him hated Cecil LeBarron for wanting what

82

he should not have, part of him hated himself for losing control of his life. He had no idea how long it took, but eventually he forced himself to let go.

"Ah, right…" Cecil finally plucked the bracelet from Gabe's rigid, half-open hand. "Thank you," he said, carefully placing it on a black velvet cushion. Reaching into his jacket he brought out an iPhone, swiped the screen and took two pictures, flash on and flash off. He pecked delicately at the screen and looked over at Gabe as the phone made its 'email sent' *whoosh* sound. "I have someone who is something of a collector of this type of thing. I told him about your visit, and he said he'd very much like to see the piece – if, or as soon as, you came back. And you can't get more 'as soon as' than instantly, can you?"

Gabe was thinking that he supposed you couldn't when Cecil's phone trilled some fancy show-tune ringtone and Cecil took the call. It didn't last long and mainly consisted of Cecil nodding and going 'Uh-huh, uh-huh…' a lot, then putting the phone down.

"He likes it very much –" Cecil nodded at the bracelet – "the piece. He wants it, and he says would you be prepared to accept seventeen fifty? One thousand, seven hundred and fifty dollars, that is?"

Gabe looked at Cecil, who was observing him with one eyebrow raised. Seventeen hundred and fifty dollars? With what he'd got from Benny that would make his total just a little shy of two grand! Something clicked in his head and he heard himself say, "This is like a *bargaining* situation, right?"

"Ah … y-e-e-s…" Cecil dragged the word out, like he was giving himself thinking time.

"You say a price, I say a price, isn't that what you said?" Gabe had never bargained in his life, but he felt weirdly like he had nothing to lose. He overrode the crawling guilt, wouldn't let himself look directly at the bracelet, just thought of all the money.

Cecil nodded. "I did, indeed."

"OK, two thousand dollars."

"Eighteen hundred."

"Nineteen hundred."

"Eighteen fifty."

"Eighteen seventy-five."

Gabe held his breath, watching Cecil watching him. Cecil broke first.

"I, ah… I can do that…" he nodded. "My client can go to eighteen seventy-five."

Gabe's mouth twitched. He'd won, though he'd

had to betray himself to do it. But everything and everyone had their price…

Cecil paid him in cash, no receipt. A simpler, neater way to do business, he'd said. *Yeah, right*, Gabe thought; a simpler, neater way not to pay taxes, more like. Eighteen hundreds, a fifty, a twenty and a five. He now had just over two thousand dollars – two *thousand* dollars! – in an envelope, hidden at the bottom of his backpack. A couple of grand. He reckoned he now knew why a grand was called that, as you did feel good when you had that much money. And now he also knew Cecil had a client who wanted what he had, and was prepared to pay for it. Which was good to know as there was more where that came from. How much would the rest of the stash be worth? The knife alone… A bad taste leaked into his mouth at the thought of selling the knife, and he took a swig from his bottle of water and spat it out to try and get rid of it. Parting with the bracelet hadn't been easy, but he'd managed it. And he would do it again, he would sell everything.

For now he had the two grand. It wasn't going to solve all his family's problems, but it would help and that was all he'd wanted to do. And then the thought struck him, straight out of left field and completely unexpected – how was he going to explain the money? What good would it be to have it if he couldn't figure out a way for the family to use it? Turning up with that much money, in cash, was going to prompt the kind of questions he did not want to answer. Why he hadn't thought about this before he didn't know, but thinking about it now sure took the shine off of the situation.

With the light beginning to fade, Gabe swung right off the main drag, Ventura Boulevard, and into the low-rise urban grid where he lived, still thinking about what he was going to do and not really paying attention. Not picking up that the street he was on was unusually quiet and empty. It was only when, out of the corner of his eye, he saw a flash of red that his personal safety radar kicked in. Baseball cap red, at baseball-cap-on-head height. Over to his left, ten, fifteen metres away...

As the figure wearing the cap and an old brown leather jacket kind of slid out of the shadows, Gabe braked hard and slewed the rear wheel of the bike round 180 degrees. The street he'd come down was completely empty and silent, apart from the blood singing wildly in his ears.

His brain scrambled to make sense of what was happening. Of what should not, could *not* be happening.

Where was everyone?

He looked desperately for a way out, but couldn't move.

What was this person going to do to him?

Fear gripped him, squeezed him like a snake. It was as if he'd switched places with the boys he'd seen being sacrificed; the inevitability of the situation, like the boys', becoming clearer by the second. He was going to die. And like the boys, his heart was going to be torn from his chest and his blood would soak into the sidewalk. His fate was sealed.

Gabe wanted to shout out for help, but it felt like he had a hand round his throat and there was this crazy idea in his head that, even if he could yell, no one would be able to hear him. The fingers of an icy chill crept out from his spine and through his body. How this man from his nightmares came to be here, on his way home, didn't make any sense. But then neither did the way he'd felt when he'd tried to hand the bracelet over to Mr LeBarron. Random thoughts cannoned into each other. No one should know how they were going to die... No kid should die before their parents did... Did you know it when you went certifiably insane?

Gabe felt himself begin to buckle under the strain of keeping himself together and waiting to see what this person did to him. He let his bike drop to the ground and turned to face the man in the faded red baseball cap, the man who was now only metres away, his face so deeply shadowed by the cap brim that Gabe couldn't make out a single feature.

There was a movement behind the old man and a coyote came into view. As it stared at him, Gabe remembered that witches and wizards always had sidekick demons, familiars that took the shape of animals. A frazzled thought crossed his mind – this was what the owl and the coyotes had to be. Demons.

Gabe tried to turn and run but only managed to shuffle back a pace or two; it was as if he'd been separated from the real world, which he could see but not reach. The man stopped, an arm's length away, and Gabe could smell him, a sharp, musty aroma crawling up his nostrils, strong enough to make him gag. He was desperate to escape at any cost, but he couldn't move.

"*Give … it all … back…*"

Chapter Eleven

The man was close enough now that Gabe could see the pores on his face, the skin brown and heavily creased like old, old leather; the voice was a hushed, scratchy whisper, rough sandpaper on even rougher wood, as if he hadn't spoken for a long time.

But his cracked, dry lips never moved.

"Give it … all … back…"

The words echoed in Gabe's brain and the only thing he could do was watch, eyes wide, as the man slowly lifted his head to look directly at him. The face staring at him was picked out by the last of the light spilling like gold dust over the urban skyline. It should have warmed his features, but instead it made the man's cheekbones and jawline sharper, his nose more beak-like. And his unblinking eyes… Gabe was mesmerized by them. Two polished black stones, each one set deep in its socket, they glowed, the fire inside pulling Gabe in.

Eyes were the windows of the soul. Gabe had heard that said, but couldn't remember when or who by. If it was true he was facing down one truly mean character. *Mean and evil*, so the tiny, scared voice in his head kept on reminding him. Gabe didn't care that the human sacrifices he'd witnessed him committing were in a dream, he knew, no shadow of a doubt, that they had happened…

"*Give it to me – I require it!*"

"I … I…" The effort of mumbling those two small words made Gabe break out into a sweat. And then the dam broke and everything poured out. "If I had it here, believe me, mister, I'd give it all to you in a *second*, I would! But I *don't* have it, OK? I don't. Not right now. But I can get it … yeah, I can… I can get it." As he spoke, Gabe could hear the desperation in his voice. *What am I saying?* he thought. *Exactly* how *am I gonna do that? Is nice Mr Cecil LeBarron just going to turn right around and sell the bracelet, on which he has no doubt made a tidy profit, back to me?* "I didn't *know* it belonged to anyone! I just found it, right? I didn't know it was yours, how could I? If I had I wouldn't have taken it, I wouldn't… It was an accident."

"*Trouble … bad trouble…*"

"Trouble? You gonna call the cops? Hey, you don't have to do that!" Gabe saw an owl land behind the coyote; he pointed at it. "Look, the damn bird was there, the coyotes too. The owl saw..."

Gabe stopped, hearing how ridiculous and close to tears he sounded. He had gone crazy, he must have. What other explanation could there be? He was seeing things, he was babbling like a loonytune and any minute now some doctor was going to jab a loaded hypodermic in him and he'd wake up somewhere strapped to a hospital bed.

"Why didn't anyone stop me?" Gabe stared, transfixed by the red glow that flared in the man's eyes.

"*It has been so long, so very long...*" Once again his lips, slightly parted to reveal a ragged collection of yellowed and uneven teeth, didn't move. "*I was not strong enough, but I am getting stronger...*"

Before Gabe had a chance to wonder how it was he could hear what the man was saying when he didn't appear to be talking, a bony, iron-hard fist slammed him in the gut. He folded over and fell to the ground, completely winded and unable to breathe, sharp stones in the asphalt biting at his face.

"*Such* bad *trouble … if I do not get it back…*"

Gabe, eyes squeezed shut, felt the man stoop over him and he flinched, waiting to be hit again. A dank smell wrapped round the whispered words fading away inside his head. In the long silence Gabe was sure he must have died, before figuring out that if you died maybe you wouldn't hurt any more…

"Gabriel? Gabriel? Are you OK? What happened?"

Stella? Gabe slowly unfolded himself. Stella was kneeling down next to him, silhouetted against the sky. How long had he been lying here?

"Did you get hit by a car? Did you see it?"

"No –" Gabe pushed himself off the ground and stood up, a little unsteady – "and no."

"You haven't broken anything, have you?" Stella reached out and touched his face. "Are you sure you're OK?"

"I'm OK… Just need a hand up…"

Chapter Twelve

Sometimes a bad thing happens, and then a good thing happens right afterwards, like a reward, or karma. Something like that. Gabe's thinking circuits were kind of blown from being bounced around. But he did know that while it was Bad to be trashed by some old dude with a real shitty attitude, it was Good being found by Stella, who had a car and hadn't minded driving him and his bike home.

Gabe thought he'd get away with Stella simply dropping him off and going on her way. No such luck. She was coming in and making sure he was all right, no argument. So it was also Good that no one was there when they walked in. Empty house, because it was parents' evening at Remy's school. Result.

"Thanks for, you know, everything, but I totally am fine." Gabe put real effort into his smile.

"Maybe you are —" Stella hung her camera bag

off the back of a chair – "but you have cuts and I have a girl-scout badge in first aid." She looked round the kitchen. "So, where's the emergency kit?"

"In the bathroom, I guess." Gabe nodded at the open door. "Turn left, at the end of the hallway."

"I'll be right back…"

Gabe sat down, watching Stella walk out the kitchen. One minute he's in the middle of a complete nightmare scenario, being floored by a sucker punch from some dude with glowing eyes, the next there's Stella, in an old silver Toyota Corolla. He was wondering just exactly how his life could get any weirder when Stella came back holding a blue box with a red cross on the lid in one hand and a small glass bottle in the other.

"Your mother has Rescue Remedy –" Stella held up the little bottle, like she'd won a prize – "and a lot of other good stuff— Now stay where you are."

Gabe, halfway to his feet, sat back down. Let her nurse him back to health, if that was what she wanted to do. Why argue with that?

A quarter of an hour later Stella had completed her clean-up-repair-and-restore job, ten minutes after that Gabe had showered, changed and put a wash on so there'd be no awkward questions about bloodstains, however minor, from his mom. The cuts and scratches he'd have to deal with. A cup of green tea was waiting for him on the table when he walked back into the kitchen, Stella sitting opposite it. He pulled out a chair, picked up the cup and had a sip.

"Thanks…"

"My pleasure, Gabriel."

Gabe concentrated on the cup in front of him, feeling like he was in court and under oath; he looked up to find Stella still looking straight at him. "What?"

"What happened out there, in the street?"

Gabe shrugged.

"Well, you didn't get knocked over by any hit-and-run driver, did you? So, was it Benny? I told you—"

"It wasn't Benny."

Gabe looked back at the cup, almost wishing it had been, or that he'd had the smarts to lie and say it was. How could he tell Stella the truth without appearing to be a complete nutjob? And of course, for all he knew, he could well *be* a complete nutjob, considering what had happened.

"Well, if it wasn't Benny, who was it?"

Just because someone asked you a question – that someone being a quite forceful, really very good-looking girl – and kind of deserved an explanation, just because of all that, didn't mean you *had* to answer if you didn't want to. And Gabe really didn't want to. There was no law. And when your back was up against the wall, you could either wave the white flag, or push. Gabe was in no mood to surrender.

"Look, I don't know who it was, OK?" Not a lie, as he didn't. "But what were you doing there anyway... You know, right place, right time? Were you like *following* me? Don't get me wrong, I'm not complaining, I'm glad you found me and, you know, gave me a ride and everything..." Gabe began to lose steam. "But ... but, like, *if* you were following me, that would be kind of weird – a bit of a pattern. Twice in a couple of days, there you are? Why do you care so much about what I do, or don't do, with that fruit loop Benny? *And* you also had my cell number, right? How'd you get that, is your dad in the CIA or the NSA or something?"

"OK… OK…"

It was Stella's turn to look away and for a moment Gabe thought, the way she was blinking her eyes, maybe he'd gone too far, been too hard on her. He *really* hoped she didn't start to cry.

"I suppose I should, you know…" Stella got her phone out of the camera bag, on the table next to her; she flicked the screen a couple of times and turned it to face Gabe. On it was a head and shoulders picture of a guy, maybe in his early twenties, slightly wavy brown hair, gold earring, one of those haven't-shaved-for-a-week beards. He was smiling and seemed to be about as happy as you could get without looking like you were putting it on. "I had a brother, Ed."

"Had?"

"He died."

"Oh … geez, I'm sorry."

"He was such a sweetheart and *such* a jerk, all wrapped up in the same person. If there was a choice to make, *any* at all, he would always find a way to make it the wrong one. He couldn't help it, it was like a personality disorder. He wasn't stupid, but he did *the* most stupid things and then wondered why shit happened to him. He never could figure out why our parents gave up on him and wouldn't carry on cutting him slack, like they always used to…"

Stella turned the phone so she could look at the picture and Gabe saw there was a tear running down her cheek. She wiped it away with the back of her hand.

"He wasn't bad, Gabe, not really. He just wouldn't listen, to anyone. And you know what? The first time I saw you, you reminded me of him in a lot of ways and for whatever reason that worried me, even though I didn't even know you…"

Gabe watched Stella draw herself back together, not knowing what to say. Had he just been insulted, or complimented? Hard to tell. Maybe he should stick to the facts and steer away from the emotional.

"How'd he die?"

"How did he die?" Stella sniffed. "Can I have a tissue or something?"

Gabe leapt up and got a roll of kitchen paper.

Stella smiled a little. "I'm not going to turn the taps on, just a sheet would have done."

"Better safe than sorry, right?"

"I suppose." Stella tore a sheet off the roll, but didn't use it. "He... Ed ... he was, um, just always in the wrong place, always hanging out with the wrong crowd. And he could never say 'no'. Short and long? He died of a drug overdose. He was only twenty-two..."

Now Stella did use the kitchen paper, burying her face in it, and Gabe had no idea what he should say or do. Reach across and comfort her? Go round the table?

"And you know who he was hanging round with?" Stella looked up, angry. There were no tears now, and she didn't wait for an answer. "Benny. Benny 'the fruit loop', right? He was working for him, running errands, doing this and that. How *dangerous* could that be, he always said? *He* knew what he was doing, he said. Just like you, Gabriel. Just like you.

"I got myself transferred to Morrison because I knew that was where the creep hung around. I wanted to see what I could find out, and what I found was you, acting just like Ed..."

Now Gabe didn't have a clue what to say. Sure, he felt like an idiot because he knew, in his heart of hearts, that having *any*thing to do with Benny was stupid, even if the money had been easy to earn. But at the same time he was having difficulty seeing where the rest of the parallels were. Some kind of response was beginning to formulate itself, along the lines of 'What makes you think *I* don't listen?' when the side door to the kitchen opened and Remy skipped in.

Chapter Thirteen

"Hey, Gabey, you had a fight or something?" Remy stopped in her tracks and transferred her laser-guided attention to Stella. "Oh, hi, are you Gabe's girlfriend?"

At which point Gabe's parents walked in.

Right at that moment every pair of eyes in the room was focused on him, as if his answer to Remy's question would undoubtedly be the solution to world hunger.

"Well, I'm a girl, and I *am* his friend –" Stella turned to look at Remy – "so, yeah, I suppose you could say that. My name's Stella, I just started in the same grade as Gabriel at Morrison. What's your name?"

"Remy."

"Nice to meet you, Remy." Stella pushed her chair back and stood up, shouldering her camera bag; she smiled at Gabe's parents, glanced back at Gabe and then at her watch. "I'm sorry, but I have to go..."

This girl, Gabe thought, watching her negotiate her way out of the kitchen, *is one smooth operator.*

"Come by tomorrow, Gabriel!" Stella waved, then disappeared out of the kitchen.

"She's nice, *Gabriel*." Remy went over to the fridge. "And she *likes* you, she really *likes* you…"

"What happened to you, Gabe?"

His mom came round the table, a concerned look on her face. His dad stayed at the door, watching him.

"I, you know, kind of skidded on some gravel, Mom –" the first thing that came into his head – "hit the brake and the back wheel went out from under me. No biggie. Really, I'm fine."

"Were you in traffic? Did you have your helmet on?" His mom peered at the right-hand side of his face. "Did your friend, did Stella clean you up?"

Gabe nodded, catching his dad watching.

"She seems very nice. How long have you…?"

"Mom!" Gabe could feel himself blushing. "Like she said, we're just friends, OK?"

Remy grinned. "She *likes* you, she really *likes* you…"

103

The ragging had continued right through dinner, which was leftovers his mom had cunningly disguised as a tasty kind of stir-fry/chow mein hybrid. After eating, Gabe bailed, saying he had schoolwork, and if he did it now then he wouldn't have to do anything on it over the weekend. When his dad still had his job, this was when he might have opened up his wallet and given him a twenty for when he went out. Not tonight.

He did have some work to do, but not for school. He needed to see if he could find out more about the pieces he'd dug up. He had pictures of everything, taken with his phone and downloaded to his laptop, and he was going to have to scout around on the Net, get creative with the questions he asked. That's what they were always being told at school, that the quality of the answers you got depended entirely on the quality of the questions you asked. G.I.G.O. His English teacher had that pinned up on the wall: Garbage In Garbage Out. It kind of made sense.

He had just started his search, pulling up a site about the Aztecs, when there was a tap on his bedroom door and his dad came straight in. He closed the door behind him and leant back against it.

This was obviously going to be Part II of the non-conversation they'd had in the kitchen yesterday. Which he could do without. So he waited, not saying anything.

Gabe's dad rubbed the bristle on his chin. "I know what you think."

"You do? About what?"

"Me."

Gabe shrugged, wondering where this was going.

"And I get why you think like that. It's not good to see your old man laid off and laid low, I understand that. Happened to your Grandad Mikey, back in the 80s, when we used to live in Detroit. Everything went to hell in a hand basket for Big Mike and he wasn't so big any more. We ended up coming out here, which I hated at the time, and hated him for making us do it. Leave all our friends, everything we knew…"

"Are you trying to break it to me that *we're* gonna have to move?"

"No, no I am not, Gabe, I'm *trying* to explain that shit happens to people and those people have to deal with it in their own way." Gabe's dad looked away from him for a second. "You might think you

105

have the picture all worked out, but my advice? Don't judge until you've been there…"

Gabe interrupted his dad again. "So what *are* you saying?"

"I'm saying, stop being such a hard-ass, Gabe. I know this is tough on you – it's tough on everyone – but don't make it any tougher by not talking. You know, or you should know, that you can talk to me about anything. We will get through this, trust me."

Gabe stared at the screensaver image in front of him. Trust. Yeah, you should be able to trust your own dad. He *wanted* to trust his dad, to talk to him. But, Gabe glanced at him, still leaning against the door, not now, not tonight. He was too tired, too wired and he just wanted to be left alone. He had work to do. And he had earned a lot of money today, unlike…

"Son?"

"Yeah, sorry…" Gabe nodded at his dad. "I get it, Dad, I do. Everything you said. I just, you know, have to get some stuff done?"

"Sure." His dad stepped over and lightly punched Gabe's arm. "Make some time over the weekend. I'll get some beers in, right?"

"Right," Gabe smiled.

He sat staring at the closed door for a long time, feeling bad about the way he'd treated his dad, wanting to go after him to apologize. Tell him they would talk, soon, that now was just so not the right time. Frustrated, Gabe hit the top of his desk with his fist, jolting the mouse and bringing up the site about the Aztecs. Back to work.

Before he went to bed, the other thing he was going to do was get one of his mom's Ambiens. He knew where she kept them. He'd only take a half of one of the sleeping pills, as he really needed to punch out and he did not want to dream. Not tonight. As he started to read what was on the screen he tried to ignore the voice that said 'sleep the sleep of the dead...'

Chapter Fourteen

Gabe brought the bike to a slow halt. It was a kind of 'What's-wrong-with-this-picture?' moment. Like what were two LAPD cruisers, lights flashing, doing parked right outside LeBarron Antiques? Had there been a robbery? The thought made his stomach cramp. It'd be just his luck that that was what had happened and the bracelet would be among the stolen items. His chances of getting Cecil LeBarron to sell it back to him – for the money he'd paid out yesterday – had been slim to nothing at best. But if the bracelet was gone, then – there was that voice again – he was dead in the water.

He got off the bike and, completely on autopilot, chained it to a nearby bench. A large crowd had gathered either side of the shop, held back by the yellow and black crime-scene tape that was already in place. More people were turning up by the minute, which meant the cops couldn't have been there very long, their arrival signalling it was rubbernecking time.

Gabe hung back, staying where he was for a moment. He wanted to find out what had occurred, but then again, maybe not knowing was better. Some part of his brain kept dragging up clichés like 'Ignorance is bliss' and 'What you don't know can't hurt you'. He took a deep breath and walked towards the store alongside two older women who were chatting to each other.

"What's going on here?" one woman said as she checked her watch.

"*I* don't know, Charlene just called."

"She down here already?"

"In the salon across the street." Gabe saw the second woman nod to her left. "She can't come out, she's in the middle of having highlights."

"So, what, you're her on-the-spot reporter, Alice?"

"You don't got to come, Sadie, I ain't draggin' you."

"It's kinda on my way." Sadie checked her watch again. "I got time. You think it's a burglary, or what?"

"I think I'm gonna ask that cop, see what he says…"

Gabe tagged along, walking in the same general direction as the women, over towards a beat cop who was standing with his back to them where the tape was tied to a tree.

"Officer?" Alice leant over and tapped the cop's arm.

The man, standing a good two metres, wearing mirrored sunglasses and carrying some extra weight, looked like his uniform had been sprayed on. He glanced down at Alice. "Yes, ma'am?"

"What's the scoop?"

"Ma'am?"

"In there." Alice peered round towards the shop. "It a big deal, in there?"

"I wouldn't know, ma'am. As you can see, I am out here."

"You didn't hear about anything?"

"Look, you want to find out what's going on in there, you have a couple of options." The cop, his name tag said 'Bernado', smiled. "Cross the line and go on inside, which I would not advise, or wait till the detectives come out and ask them. And good luck with that too. Or wait for the six o'clock news. Best I can do."

Officer Bernardo smiled again and walked away. Gabe was thinking he should get closer to the shop front, keeping his ears open in case anyone had actually heard anything, when he saw, over by one of the cruisers, a plain-clothes cop talking to a small Hispanic woman. She looked distressed and the plain-clothes cop was patting her arm, trying to calm her. A witness?

That train of thought came to an abrupt halt, cut off by the whooping of an ambulance siren. The crowd buzzed with chatter, moving forward as far as it could. Officer Bernardo and three of his colleagues squared their shoulders and made sure the lines held.

The ambulance pulled up, rocking on its suspension and Gabe watched as a couple of EMT paramedics got out, already pulling on latex gloves. They went round to the rear of the vehicle and hauled out a gurney, locking its legs and wheeling it towards the open front door of the shop.

"Someone ain't gonna walk outta *that* place, you ask me," said a man next to Gabe.

"No shit, Sherlock," the guy next to him laughed.

"You heard what happened?" Gabe threw the question out, to no one in particular.

"Likely a burglary gone bad," the laughing guy said. "Looking at the amount of heat there is here."

"Opening-up time," the first man nodded to himself. "It's when they like to do it, burglars."

"Say what?" the second man snorted. "So's they get the rest of the day off?"

Right then there was a flurry of activity, another push from the crowd and Gabe saw the gurney being rolled back out on to the sidewalk. He was expecting to see Cecil LeBarron, covered in one of those foil survival blankets, looking maybe a bit beaten up and washed out, despite his fake tan, being taken off to the Emergency Room. Instead he saw a zipped-up black body bag.

"You hear me, right?" said the man, turning to the guy who'd laughed at him, a told-you-so look on his face.

"You mentioned walking, man, you never said nothing about *dead*."

Cecil LeBarron was dead? Gabe couldn't quite take the information in. Then it occurred to him that he didn't know for sure it was Cecil in the body bag. Could be the burglar, right? Cecil could come walking out of the store any minute now. Except

112

Mr LeBarron hadn't really come across as the fight-back type. The next person to exit the antique store was a second plain-clothes guy, Gabe assumed he was another detective, on his phone.

"The owner? He's on his way to the morgue now… LeBarron." The man checked a notepad as he spelt the surname out. "Yeah, yeah, we'll stay here, wait for the crime-scene guys to finish, see if they come up with anything that could…"

Whatever else the man had to say was lost as he walked over to where his colleague was still interviewing the Hispanic woman. No doubt about it now. Cecil was dead. Gabe felt a little lightheaded, spaced out by what he'd just seen and heard and what it meant. Or *could* mean. He *could* be jumping to conclusions, thinking this had anything at all to do with the gold bracelet he'd sold yesterday. The bracelet he'd come to try and buy back because of some crazed person with weird eyes who had beat the crap out of him. And threatened him with, what had he said? Bad trouble? Ending up dead was about as bad as trouble got, and he had no difficulty believing the crazy man was a killer, even if his only proof was a dream.

But why would he have killed Mr LeBarron? He'd seen Gabe coming out of the store, which is how he'd known about the place, but *how* did he know the bracelet was there? Why kill the man, why not simply take the gold and go?

Gabe knew he wasn't thinking straight, hadn't been since he tumbled into the arroyo and found the gold, and he wondered if he might be suffering from some kind of concussion. What did he know?

It took a moment for Gabe to realize that he'd smelled something, something pungent and musty. He glanced left and right, then looked over his shoulder. The peak of a faded red baseball cap, close up behind him.

"Treasures gained by wickedness do not profit," the whispered croak of the man's voice rasped, *"but righteousness delivers from death…"*

Wheeling round, his heart thundering, Gabe found the man looking straight at him. It was just like yesterday – all he could hear was the echo of the man's words in his head. He closed his eyes, waiting for the punch he assumed was coming. When it didn't and he blinked them open again, the man had gone and there was just some woman trying to get a better view of what was going on.

Gabe, his breath coming in short pants, thought he saw a red cap somewhere in the crowd. And then he became aware there was something in his right hand. Looking down he saw a small square of yellowing paper, neatly folded twice. The paper looked old and felt stiff as he opened it out. There was some writing in what appeared to be dark brown ink. Writing in the kind of style you associated with quill pens, ancient documents and wax seals.

Six words. *Quod meum est mei, noli prohibere.*

Chapter Fifteen

Gabe walked away from the antique store in a daze. Everything else around him had faded away, all airbrushed out. He hadn't been imagining it, every move he made was being watched, and the man watching could get to him wherever he was, awake or asleep. He started to wonder whether it was stupid or not to think his dreams and his reality were beginning to merge, then he remembered another line he'd read in one of his dad's old comics, some character saying, 'Just cos yer paranoid don't mean they ain't after you'.

Well, they – the killer priest person, the owl and the coyotes – were definitely after him, and too right he was paranoid. With that weird musty smell still clinging to his nostrils, why wouldn't he be?

Walking back to where he'd left his bike, Gabe kept returning to the fact that Cecil LeBarron was dead. As in definitely not alive. True fact. And what he also knew to be true was that he wasn't suffering from a concussion and had not been hallucinating. This was real. He glanced at the piece of paper again, then refolded it and stuffed it in his jeans pocket. What did the words mean – hell, what *language* were they even written in? And what had the guy meant by righteousness delivering from death?

He stood by his bike, staring blankly into space. How was he going to find out what had happened to the bracelet? Going to the police was not an option, as what would he say if they asked where he'd got an antique gold bracelet in the first place? And how could he ever tell the cops about this crazy person being the one who had killed Cecil? He couldn't, it wasn't going to happen.

But there was a harder question to deal with. Was there some kind of deadline he didn't know about attached to returning the rest of the gold? If there was it had to mean he was in … 'dead trouble' came to mind and wouldn't go away.

The rest of the gold pieces were at school, in his locker, and it was Saturday. No way he could get in to fetch it till Monday morning at the earliest. He unlocked the bike and put the chain in his backpack, on top of the envelope with the money in it. The two thousand dollars. Was it blood money? Tainted? That thought sent his mind spinning into turmoil again as he tried to figure out what he should do next.

The only thing he knew for sure was that he badly needed to talk to someone. And the only person he could think of was Stella. Who else was there? Anton? He didn't think so. Ant was a good friend – no, he was his *best* friend – but the chances he might act like Gabe was making all this up, like it was some huge practical joke he was playing, were too big to take. And the rest of his friends would be worse. It had to be Stella. Firstly, she'd asked him to call her today. Secondly, she already suspected his story about being knocked over by a car was a load of bull and, finally, she had been so honest with him about her brother. So he should be as honest with her. *Quid pro quo*. The phrase stopped Gabe in his tracks, midway through shouldering his backpack.

The words on the paper. He couldn't be totally sure, but he had a strong feeling they were Latin. A dead language…

It had taken him a lifetime to decide whether he should bring something with him or not. Having figured he should, he was then faced with the nightmare of choosing what that something should be. Flowers? Oh, puh-leeze. Box of chocolates? Ditto. In the end he plumped for an XXL-sized bag of peanut M&M's. It was a test. If she hated them they were destined never to be anything more than acquaintances. Following the instructions Stella had given him when he'd called her, Gabe had gone round the house to the back porch.

The house looked sort of like his, except bigger, more recently painted, with a very nice pool that took up a lot of the back yard. The place wasn't a McMansion, nothing like it, but it didn't look as if Stella's dad was trying to work out what his next move in the job market might be. Before he had a chance to pull back the screen door, the kitchen door opened.

"Hey! You all right, Gabriel?" Stella waved Gabe in and let the screen door slam behind him. "You look kind of, I don't know, worried?"

119

"No… No, I'm fine."

"OK."

Stella went over to the fridge, Gabe just knowing she wasn't buying into his 'I'm fine' schtick. He had no idea he was that transparent.

"Want an ice tea?"

"Yeah, thanks, that'd be great."

"Are you sure you—"

"Look, I've got to…" Gabe smiled and shook his head. "Sorry, I butted in – you first."

"I was just going to say are you sure you're OK, cos I think you look, I don't know… Like you've had a scare?"

Gabe sighed and nodded. This girl was witchy, but maybe that was the kind of person he could use on his side right now. "Yeah, well, I was going to say that I, you know, needed to talk about some stuff. If that's OK…"

"Sure." Stella poured two glasses of ice tea. "Like about what happened yesterday?"

"Kind of…" Gabe felt he was about to jump off a cliff. It was a now-or-never moment. "You know the canyon, the one a couple of miles down Ventura?"

Chapter Sixteen

It was crazy how elastic time could be. Slowing down to nothing, if you were bored, or speeding up if you had too much to do or say. Gabe had started talking in the kitchen, carried on as they went to Stella's room and not stopped until he'd told her every last detail he could remember. By the time he'd described what had just happened outside the antique store the clock on Stella's desk claimed he'd been talking for some forty-five minutes, but it had seemed like no time at all. And Stella hadn't said a single word throughout, just listened intently.

Gabe, sitting cross-legged on the floor a metre away from Stella, stared at the open but untouched pack of M&M's. Finally he looked up and shrugged in a 'that's it, whaddya think?' kind of way. If he'd believed in the power of prayer he would have been in full 'Oh, Lord!' mode as if his life depended on it. Instead, all he could do was hope she didn't think he was crazy and ask him to leave and never come back.

He watched the clock tick.

Stella kind of smiled at him.

Was that it? Was that a goodbye look?

"Know what?" Gabe grabbed the moment before Stella had a chance to say anything. "Can we go outside? I could do with some fresh air after that talkathon."

"Sure." Stella got up.

"So you, like, don't think I'm crazy?"

"No. No, I don't." Stella went to the door. "I think you need some help."

"So you *do* think I'm nuts."

"No, Gabriel, I don't."

Gabe picked up the untouched M&M's. "Maybe these'll help us figure out what it says on that piece of paper. You got any ideas?"

"No —" she led the way downstairs — "but I'd like another look at the pics on your phone."

Gabe followed Stella out of the house and down to the end of the garden, beyond the pool, where there was a wooden bench and table shaded by a tall, broad dogwood tree. It didn't take long to go

122

through the pictures Gabe had taken of the gold pieces, or to make major inroads into the M&M's. Stella, it turned out, was a fellow devotee.

"I think you're probably right about those words being written in Latin, Gabe."

OK, so he was 'Gabe' now.

"And I had an idea, because of that cross you found with the other stuff? It made me think of this person I know, who's big into history and everything; I think he might be able to help." Stella took another handful of M&M's. "Now I've seen the photos again, I'm sure he can. Really."

"Who is this guy, some kind of genius?"

"Father Simon."

Chapter Seventeen

Father Simon, the priest at Sacred Heart, the church Stella's family went to, lived in the rectory, a large, two-storey building next to the church grounds. Stella pulled up outside, put the Toyota in 'Park' and switched the engine off.

"OK –" she started to get out of the car – "let's see what he has to say."

"He won't mind me not being Catholic, right?"

"He won't mind, and he won't try and convert you, either. At least not straight away." Stella caught the look on Gabe's face and laughed. "Just kidding. He's cool."

"For a priest?"

"For anyone."

The door was answered by a woman, which surprised Gabe, for a second making him think, *Is this priest* married?

"Hi, Mrs Callaghan," Stella said. "We phoned

earlier, Father Simon is expecting us."

The woman, Gabe had worked out she must be some sort of housekeeper, showed them in and took them down the hallway to a back room with French windows that looked out on to a mid-sized garden, all lawn, with high cypress hedges. A man, frizzy white hair and gold-rimmed glasses, dressed all in black with a white back-to-front collar, looked up from his desk as they walked in.

"Ah, thank you, Mrs Callaghan, thank you."

Mrs Callaghan hovered by the door. "Your supper's in the fridge, Father, so I'll be going, if that's all right."

"That's completely fine –" Father Simon smiled, his face creased with arcs of laughter lines – "and I will see you tomorrow."

The priest got up, seeming shorter than he'd looked sitting at his desk, and walked across the room to an armchair, waving at the sofa that faced the French windows. The light from outside shone through his shock of unruly, thinning white hair, turning it into a wiry halo.

"Sit down, sit down." He followed his own advice. "And so, Stella my dear, how can I help?"

"This is Gabe, Father, Gabriel Mason, a friend of mine." Stella sat one end of the sofa, Gabe went to the other, further away from Father Simon. "He's found some things and I hope you may be able to figure out what they are."

"Nice to meet you, Gabriel." Father Simon got up and stuck out his hand. Gabe had no choice but to get up himself, lean across the table between them and do the same, and they shook hands awkwardly. "So, what have you found?"

Gabe glanced at Stella, then got out his phone and brought up the first picture of the gold pieces he'd taken from the skeleton. He handed the phone to Stella, who leant over and showed the picture to Father Simon, then gave him the phone.

"You know how to swipe and everything, Father?"

"I may seem very last-century, but I keep up." The priest spent a few minutes looking at the pictures, closely examining one in particular before he put the phone down on the table. "Very, uh, interesting... Where did they come from, these items?"

Stella looked pointedly at Gabe, the silent message being, 'Your turn, guy'.

"I, y'know, I found them, ah..." Gabe couldn't

quite bring himself to say 'Father'. He didn't call his own father Father.

"We can cut the formalities here. Call me Simon, or Mr Murrow, if you like; whatever makes you comfortable,"

"OK, ah, Simon… I found them, buried with this old skeleton up in a canyon off Ventura." Gabe leant forward, elbows on knees.

"*Exactly* like they are here?"

"I washed the dirt off, that's all."

"And the cross, that's how it was when you found it?"

Gabe shrugged. "Sure."

Father Simon picked up the phone and sat back in his chair, flicking through the photos again. Gabe tried to read the expression on the man's face, but all he could get was a sense that he was worried. Which was not what Gabe wanted to see.

"Is there anything else, Gabriel?"

"I guess, but I didn't have the tools with me to do any more digging, but—"

"No, no – I meant apart from the gold."

"Yeah… Yeah, there is." Gabe stood up, retrieved the square of paper from his pocket and handed it over. Father Simon unfolded it very carefully, frowning as he did so.

"Parchment … the real deal too, I'd say."

Gabe leant forward. "Parchment? Cooking paper?"

"No, son, writing paper, or at least writing *material* made from animal skin. This is old. Where did you get it?"

"A person, some guy, gave it to me." Gabe flicked a glance at Stella. "Today, earlier today."

"Do you know this person?"

"Not really, I've just seen him a couple of times…"

"He beat Gabe up, Father," Stella cut in. "I found him just after it'd happened."

"I see…" Father Simon looked back at the piece of paper.

"Do you know what it says, ah, Simon?"

Father Simon nodded. "I do, Gabe, and if they still taught Latin in schools today, you two might have been able to work it out for yourselves: *Quod meum est mei, noli prohibere…* What is mine is mine, do not withhold." He got up and went to his desk, his back to them as he rummaged in a drawer until he found what he wanted. He turned back with a magnifying glass in hand, angling the paper towards the window as he examined it.

"What, um… What does that mean?"

Father Simon swivelled round his office chair and sat down. He collected various items out of drawers in his desk, setting them up in front of him, and switched on an LED desk light. "It means exactly what it says, Gabe. It's a statement, a demand and a threat, all rolled into one neat little sentence."

Stella got up from the sofa and went to stand next to the priest. After a moment's hesitation, Gabe followed suit. He watched the priest as he used something that looked exactly like a surgeon's scalpel to gently scrape a tiny amount of ink from the paper into a glass vial. He then added a few drops of three different colourless liquids, shaking the vial after each addition.

Stella leant closer. "What are you doing, Father?"

"Mixing the sample you saw me scrape off the parchment with isopropyl alcohol, phenolphthalein, and hydrogen peroxide." Father Simon shook the vial one last time and held it up; the liquid had turned a delicate shade of pink. "As you may know, what I used to do for a living is now my hobby. You can take the man out of the crime lab, but you can't take, etc, etc."

"You were a CSI?" Gabe couldn't hide his surprise. "How…"

"How did this happen?" Father Simon pointed at his collar. "When you've seen the things I've seen, Gabe, you can't help but end up believing in true evil … the devil. I couldn't, anyway, which means you also have to take on board the *other* side of the equation. I saw the darkest of the dark side, and then I saw the light. You could say."

"So what's the test for, Father?"

"Blood, Stella. And it's positive."

Chapter Eighteen

Gabe froze. The note – this all-in-one statement/demand/threat – was written in blood? What he'd assumed was brown ink was *blood*?

Regular people didn't get given threatening notes written on pieces of old parchment in blood, or in Latin; definitely not both. At least not normal, sane, regular people. On top of Cecil LeBarron's murder, this was really creeping him out. He went and sat back down on the sofa and stared out into the garden, not actually looking at anything, just thinking. Thinking, *How could this be happening to me? What did I do?* He felt a hand on his shoulder as he kept repeating to himself that he'd found the gold, not stolen it … found the gold, not stolen it … found…

"Gabe, are you OK?"

A sense of déjà vu washed over him, hearing Stella's voice, just like the day before when she'd had to scrape him off the street. He clicked back out of his trance and blinked up at her.

"Yeah, I'm fine … just a bit…" he wiped his mouth on the back of his hand and saw the concerned look on Father Simon's face. "It was a shock, you know? The blood thing? That's all."

"I'll get you a glass of water, Gabe."

As Stella left the room, Father Simon stood up and went over to a cabinet. He got out a bottle of bourbon and a small shot glass, which he put on the table.

"Purely medicinal." He uncorked the bottle and poured a finger height and handed it to Gabe. "Water's fine, if all you are is thirsty, but I have found that a shot of Kentucky straight not only greases the wheels and oils the engine, it calms the nerves a whole lot better. Knock it back, son."

"Really?"

"Really." Father Simon put the bottle away, watching Gabe drink the small shot of bourbon down in one, screwing up his face as he did so. "An acquired taste, like most of the best things in life. Now, Gabriel –" the Father stood, his arms crossed, looking down at Gabe – "I think you already have an idea that this situation you find yourself in is serious, and from what I've seen, you are correct…"

Stella came back in with a glass of water, which she gave to Gabe before sitting down. "Sorry, have I interrupted?"

"Not a problem, I was just saying that this *is* serious, and if I am to help here, you –" he looked pointedly at Gabe – "have to tell me everything. Every little thing, son."

For the second time that day Gabe started with how he'd discovered the skeleton and finished outside Cecil LeBarron's antique store, where he'd found the piece of paper in his hand. Like when he'd told Stella, laying the facts out in a logical order, crazy though they seemed, had a calming effect on him. Nothing made any more sense the second time round, but talking about it to another person, especially someone like this Father Simon, was good. Really good.

"So, what d'you think, Father?"

"I think young Gabe here has inadvertently jabbed a big stick into a wasps' nest, Stella." The Father got up and went to the bookshelves lining the wall behind him. "Tell me again what happened when you found the first piece of gold, would you? I don't recall you saying if you were standing or sitting or what."

"I was..." Gabe thought for a second, recreating the scene in his head. "Yeah, I think I was kneeling down ... that's right, I was. And I remember now, I was really hoping that the bracelet was, you know, special ... that finding it would make a difference... I wanted it to make things better, be a chance for a new start. At least be the start of a new start, right?"

"If you'd been in a church, it might have been said that you were praying." Father Simon found the book he was looking for, took it off the shelf and went back to his armchair. "And unfortunately, I have a feeling your prayers may have gotten an unwanted answer."

In the silence Gabe felt his scalp contract, and he shivered. "What d'you mean?"

"As I was saying to you before: to be able to believe in God, you also have to believe in the devil." He held out his right hand. "Dexter –" he then held out his left hand – "and sinister. Good and evil, light and dark ... the Yin and the Yang, as Confucius would put it. And while my church, and its adherents, has always tried to walk a righteous path there have been those, more than a few, no point in denying it, who have chosen to go the opposite way." Father Simon paused.

"I believe you found the last resting place of one such person. A man once of the cloth, as I think the crucifix seems to suggest, buried in unconsecrated ground, along with some shall we say *interesting* earthly belongings … all of which are intact, except for the cross. One has to ask why? What could he, and it, have done to deserve such treatment?"

"This all happened way back, right?"

"It did, Gabe, way back." Father Simon flicked through the book. "I suppose you could say it all began with the Spanish, and particularly Cortés, who was responsible for asking for Franciscan priests to be sent from Spain to convert the indigenous people to Christianity. The first to arrive, in 1524, were called The Twelve Apostles of Mexico. After Cortés had destroyed the Aztec empire he moved northwards – made the Baja some time around 1530, if my memory serves.

"But it took another two hundred years, give or take, for the Spanish to settle here, in what they called Alta California; it was sometime in the mid to late 1700s that they set up the first missions."

"You think that's when this person I found died and was buried?"

"I have a feeling this man did not die a natural death, Gabe. And if I was able to get his remains into a lab there's an outside chance I *might* have a better idea how he did meet his end."

"I wonder who he was."

"That I don't know, yet –" Father Simon tapped the book on his lap – "but I'm not just a forensic scientist, I am also something of a forensic historian. Someone like this person may well have left a trail, and if he has, I will find it.

"I'm no expert, but after what you told me about your dreams, the gold pieces could well be Aztec... That does look very much like a ritual knife. But it's the cross that really interests me. If you look carefully at the picture, there's a ring at the top so it can be hung from a chain, yes?"

Gabe swiped to the picture he'd taken of the cross and nodded.

"The way you took the shot, you can see there's also a hole at the bottom. This cross could be, and most probably was, worn hung upside down…"

"Oh my…" Gabe's eyes widened as an image flashed in his head.

"Son?" Father Simon looked at Gabe, all the colour drained from his face. "Are you OK?"

"In my dream, just before I woke up … I remember now, the guy with the knife was wearing a cross, and I thought there was something odd about it…" Gabe sat back on the sofa.

"What was it?" asked the Father. "What did you see?"

"I'm sure it was hanging upside down," Gabe said. "Why would he do that to it?"

"I believe because he worshipped false gods, including the Fallen Angel."

Gabe sat forward again and rubbed his face. He was hungry, he was confused and more than a bit freaked out. "Sorry, but in my house we've never really done church and stuff," he shrugged. "Not my parents' thing, I guess … so this all sounds, you know, kind of way out there? I mean, I've kicked around some loopy ideas since this all started and just told myself to grow up and shut it with all the Halloween nonsense. Ghosties and ghouls, right?

But you're telling me all this good and evil and worshipping fallen angels, this is for real? Who is this guy? Some kind of, I don't know, evil living dead reincarnation?"

Father Simon pursed his lips, stony-faced, and didn't say anything.

"Father?" Stella sounded scared, which spooked Gabe.

"Look –" Father Simon took a deep breath – "there have been a lot of claimants to the title of The One True Church. I believe it is mine, a belief which I am truly convinced has saved my eternal soul, but over the centuries many hundreds of thousands of people, probably millions, have died because their own beliefs differed from others. Not because they were wrong, just different, one religion's adherent being another's infidel. At another time, in another place, that could have happened to me.

"But the truth is that you can't destroy beliefs that have deep roots; the harder you try the more they cling on. They might appear to fade away, but they will continue as obscure sects and cults. Religious belief is a powerful thing – a weapon or a comfort, depending on whose hands it is in –

and the more I think about this heretic man, with his ancient gold and perverted crucifix, the more I think there were things he knew, things he did, that no man should. That's why they, whoever they were, killed him."

"And he's back?" Gabe looked out into the garden. "You think *I* brought him back?"

"I'd like nothing more than to be proved wrong, but I think it's possible. The antique store? That was no burglary gone wrong, and if I thought for one minute that it would be any use taking this note down to the station house – getting them to check the blood it's written in against the store owner's for a match – I'd run it straight down there right now."

"But you're, like, an ex-cop –" Gabe looked surprised – "why *wouldn't* they listen to you?"

"Because I'm an ex-cop, they'd listen, but I very much doubt they would take what I had to say seriously. Not until it was too late."

"Too late for what, Father?" There was that nervous edge to Stella's voice again.

"You think I'm gonna die, don't you?" Gabe couldn't believe what he'd just heard himself say, but he knew it was true. That was what the priest believed.

"I think anyone who has any of the gold in their possession is in grave danger, is what I think, Gabe."

"But he doesn't *have* the gold in his possession, Father. It's in his locker at school, remember?"

"*Quod meum est mei, noli prohibere...* What is mine is mine, do not withhold." Father Simon pushed his glasses back up his nose. "Remember? Monday, you need to get everything you took from that skeleton and bring it here to me."

"What'll you do with it? Why won't *you* be in just as much trouble as me and Cecil LeBarron?"

"Because I have faith that I can stop this."

"But what am *I* supposed to do till Monday?"

"I'll give you something..."

Chapter Nineteen

Gabe sat in the Toyota, numb. A small gold crucifix, hidden by his T-shirt, hung round his neck on a fine gold chain. Father Simon had made him promise not to take it off. So much for not being converted. Truth to tell, religion 'not being his parents' thing' was underplaying it more than slightly; if his parents saw it they'd think he'd gone nuts. His opinion, right now? He'd give anything a try.

He and Stella didn't talk much on the way back to her house. Was there anything to say that wouldn't make them feel worse? Not really. But Stella, it seemed, had used the journey as thinking time. Pulling up on her driveway she turned to Gabe.

"I have an idea — why don't we meet up later, kind of like six thirty, seven o'clock?"

"Sure…" Gabe was caught off guard, but not so much that he couldn't help but slap a grin on his face at the offer. "Where?"

"That pizza place, you know, the one on the corner of Woodman?"

"Yeah, OK, it's a deal," said Gabe thinking, *but is it a date?* "See ya there."

The whole bike ride home his head was a mess. Way too many things to think about. All he really wanted to do was play out what it would be like, meeting up with Stella later on, which as ideas went was a pretty good one in his opinion. But other thoughts kept pushing forward and getting in the way. Like the fact that he was wearing a freaking crucifix to protect himself against some risen-from–the-dead, Devil-worshipping Spanish guy. Because that *really* was going to work.

Trying not to get totalled by some lame-brain driver on his cell phone, who thought wing mirrors were for decoration, at the same time as dealing with conflicting trains of thought kept Gabe fully occupied. So much so that it took him a moment to realize that someone on a scooter was riding right next to him, keeping pace. He glanced over, wondering why whoever it was didn't just accelerate past him, and saw it was Anton on his black Vespa.

"Pull over, man…" Anton shouted, pointing at the kerb.

Gabe had no choice but do as his friend asked. He didn't want to stop and talk. He wanted to get home and get ready to go and meet Stella. But he knew he'd already stepped way beyond the mark with Anton, kept him at a distance when he should've let him in on what was happening. Pushed him away, and frozen him out.

He checked over his shoulder, braked and eased into the next parking space that came along. Anton pulled in behind him, killed the Vespa and took off his open-face helmet, rubbing his head.

"Man, you are one hard dude to track down lately."

"Yeah, I know… Sorry, Ant." Gabe was uncomfortably aware of what was hanging round his neck; he hoped Anton didn't notice the cross, or his antsyness. "What's up?"

"Kinda what I wanted to ask you, bro." Anton put his helmet over one of the Vespa's wing mirrors. "I know *some*thing's up, and I figure, if I want you to be honest with me, I gotta be honest with you, right?"

"OK…" Gabe half smiled, wondering where this was all going.

"So, it's like this…" Anton looked away, cracking his knuckles. "I didn't exactly *follow* you the other day, not like as in I was trying to spy on you, right? But when I came out of school late and saw you going off with some beardy, long-haired guy…"

"You *followed* me?"

Anton shrugged. "Hey, you looked like, I don't know, like you could be in trouble, like you might need someone with your back. So, yeah, I followed you. Saw you with that oxygen thief Benny Gueterro, getting in his van…"

"Aw, geez."

"C'mon, man … a problem shared, right?" Anton pulled the scooter back on to its stand and walked towards Gabe. "I can help, with Benny, anyway. You probably don't need any when it comes to that Stella chick…"

"*What?*"

"Look, soon as I saw you with her, bro, I went –" Anton held his hands up – "Scout's honour, man, you *know* I'm no sleezoid peep-show weirdo. I just want you to tell me what the hell you're doing in

144

spitting distance of that Benny guy, I mean, how bad can it be? We're the Two Musketeers, right, Gabe? Always have been, since forever."

Gabe stared at Anton and realized this was the same situation he'd been in with his dad, and he was feeling the same way; help was being offered, no strings attached, and all he was able to do was turn it down. With his dad he just hadn't had the right words to say what he wanted to say; with Ant, he didn't want to get his friend involved in the freak show his life was becoming. As he searched for a way out, any way out, his phone started to vibrate and ring in his pocket.

"You want to get that?" Anton looked away.

"No." Gabe waited and let the call go to voicemail. "You are gonna *have* to trust me, Ant. Trust me when I say you can't help. You really can't, not right now. And I *will* tell you what the hell is going on as soon as I can, I promise…"

Anton walked back to the Vespa, put on his helmet and sat astride the scooter. He pressed the electric starter, revved the engine, then pushed the Vespa forward, off its stand, and rode away without a word.

Gabe watched him disappear into traffic as he got out his phone. Whoever had called had left a voicemail and he automatically pressed playback and listened to the robo-voice telling him he had one new message. Then Benny started talking and didn't stop. "*You think I'm blind, maybe, Gabriel? Like what are you doing, hanging round with Eddy's kid sister? What? I got eyes around the place, Gabriel. If it's going on, I know about it, so don't try and pull the wool with me, OK? Eddy Grainger, right? Kid sister's Estelle or something… Stella. If I was playing nice, OK? If I was, I'd say I'd prefer it if you did not hang round with the broad. But I ain't doing nice today, so back off, Gabriel, capiche? Do not go there, right? Or else.*"

Gabe was having a tough enough time adjusting to the way his life was playing without Benny turning all mafia don on him. Was he being *threatened*, with the 'or else' again? He wanted to ring Benny back and ask him what his problem was with Stella, but he thought better of it.

Stella must have been *very* careless for Benny, not the sharpest knife in the drawer by a long stretch, to have found out she was doing whatever she was doing. Gabe had no idea what that might be, but he had no doubts she should cease and desist right away. He rang Stella, but the call went straight to voicemail and he mumbled something inane, about how she should call him back as soon as she got the message, and cut off.

As if his life wasn't complicated enough, as if he wasn't *paranoid* enough, he now had to worry about Stella, and whether meeting up with her in a couple of hours time was going to be cool. He found it difficult – strike that, he found it impossible to believe that Benny had a network of informants all over the Valley reporting back to him. He was a low-level dirtbag with muscle for brains, so he'd either found out by accident or, for some reason, he'd been having Stella watched. 24/7? Would he do that? Unlikely. But was it worth the risk, thinking that he wouldn't?

Gabe pushed his bike down the sidewalk. His life was unravelling. It had become a never-ending parade of unanswered and often unanswerable questions and worrying about them was screwing with his head. The irony hit him that worry, specifically about how he was going to try and help fix his family's situation, was kind of what had got him into this mess in the first place.

As he walked he texted Stella: *Benny watching u – careful yr not followed tonite*. Gabe wondered how come, if Benny really was such a moron, he'd managed to stay out of jail for so long. And what did it say about *him*, the almost-straight-A student who worked for the guy? Who, out of the two of them, was the biggest loser?

A light breeze blew in, bringing with it the kind of comforting smell of a garden trash fire. Following on, underneath those top notes, came something heavier and more earthy. For a second it didn't mean anything to Gabe, then, as if he was sampling a perfume, trying to work out its different components, he took a deeper breath and it clicked.

His hand flew up, grabbing his T-shirt, the sharp edges of the small gold cross digging into his palm, and he whirled round, expecting to find the old man in the faded red baseball cap right behind him.

He was nowhere to be seen.

Standing alone in the street, normal, ordinary life going on all around him as if everything was totally fine, Gabe didn't know how much more of this he could take. He wished he could go back a few days, to when all he had on his mind was getting through a Time of No Money; how simple did that seem now? Monday, when he could get the stash in his locker and give it to Father Simon, looked a long, long way off.

Anything could happen between now and then. The quiet voice from the dark place in his head reminded him, as if he needed it, that that also included him dying.

Chapter Twenty

"You want to do *what*?"

Gabe and Stella were sitting at a corner table, right at the back of The Pizza Parlor. Under other circumstances it might have been the romantic choice, the place for a private tête-à-tête, but not tonight. Stella, hair up and wearing a beret, sat with her back to the rest of the room. She looked different, but it was no disguise. His attempt at being incognito had been riding every back double he knew to the restaurant with his hoodie up. He'd pushed it off his head as soon as he'd arrived, not wanting to look ridiculous. They'd done the best they could.

"Go over to Morrison tonight, OK?" Gabe took a sip of his Pepsi. "I mean, why wait till Monday, right? Do it now and I get my life back. You got a better idea?"

Stella looked like she didn't know where to start, and then couldn't anyway until the waitress, who'd just appeared, had delivered their order.

"You want to break in? To the *school*?" She leant over the table, whispering. "Are you *crazy*? I know I'm new to the place, but even *I* know it's got security up the wazoo since a bunch of tech was stolen last year. Maybe you didn't hear yet..."

"Sure I know. I'm not a complete doofus."

Stella smiled. "And I know that."

"You do – how?"

"I know you a *lot* better than you know me. I've watched you." Stella took a bite of her slice.

"You stalked me?"

Stella rolled her eyes. "No! Like not *as such*, just kinda sussed you out, but when we met the other day? You didn't really have much of a clue who I was, did you? Took a moment to place me, didn't it?"

"Yeah..." No point in denying it. "Seen you around, but, you know..."

Stella took another bite, Gabe getting started with his slice. "So, tell me, Gabe, what's the plan? How're you going to get into school?"

"OK..." Gabe bit off a real big mouthful, buying some more time to think on his feet and sort out the tiny germ of an idea that had occurred to him on the ride there. "I never did it myself, but I was told there was a way in, through a window in a storeroom. It doesn't shut properly. Apparently."

"You're going to risk doing this because there's *apparently* a way in? Isn't the system supposed to be computer-controlled?"

"Yeah, but this one window doesn't have the gizmos on it, you know, the little electronic things which tell the computer what's open and what's closed? Or it has them, and they weren't wired up right and don't work. Like that."

Gabe leant an elbow on the table and cupped his chin. This was one of those friend-of-a-friend stories he thought maybe he'd heard from Anton. He didn't remember. But it didn't matter where it came from because, listening to himself, he kind of agreed with the look of disbelief on Stella's face which said it all. This wasn't a plan, it was sheer stupidity. Except, Gabe squared his shoulders, it was the only stupid plan he had and the thought of doing nothing until Monday was driving him crazy.

"You're gonna go, aren't you?"

"Sure." Gabe slumped back in his chair. "Can't sit

around and wait."

"I'm coming with you."

It was Gabe's turn to look incredulous.

"No arguments." Stella shook her head. "You'll need a lookout, backup, whatever... Gabe, you wouldn't be thinking about this if I hadn't taken you to meet Father Simon. I'm responsible."

"No, you're—"

"Yes, I am."

The girl sounded so confident, so like she had made up her mind, and that was that. Breaking into the school hadn't been how he'd intended to spend his first date with Stella, but it looked like he wasn't going to have a choice. On top of everything else he had to deal with, having Stella with him would be extra pressure. Except, if it all worked out, the worst of the hassle he was getting – the you-could-end-up-dead part – would go away.

"Penny for them, Gabe?"

"Look, Stella..." Gabe made a thing of swirling the ice in his 7Up with the straw; they both knew he was playing for time. "OK, see, it's like this. Here we are, making a lame-assed attempt to keep off of Benny's radar because he thinks he owns me and, for some reason he wouldn't say, *you* are a no-go zone. And I am wearing a freaking cross to ward off the walking dead. So us breaking into Morrison to get the stuff from my locker was not the top of my 'To Do' list. And I *am* glad you're coming with me…"

"But?"

"OK, yeah … but why *is* Benny so fired up about you, anyway?"

It was Stella's turn to take a moment, rearranging the pepperoni on her slice.

"I was careless … he saw me taking pictures."

Gabe watched as she kept on with the pepperoni rejigging, thinking, *OK, so I got that much right.*

She took a deep breath. "I never believed Ed died of an 'accidental overdose', like they said. For a start, he wasn't a user, I know he wasn't. Someone did that to him. *I* think *Benny* did that to him, for some reason, and I want him to pay for that."

Benny? Gabe couldn't get his head round the idea of him as a killer. Sure, he could be mean as a snake, and would no doubt hurt any number of flies, given half a chance, but murder?

"Why would he want to kill your brother?"

"Oh, *I* don't know, Gabe … maybe that's what

154

I'm *trying* to find out?"

Stella's angry sarcasm almost physically pushed Gabe back in his chair.

"Gabe, Gabe – I'm *so* sorry, I didn't mean..." Stella reached across the table, squeezed Gabe's hand and wouldn't let go. "It's been such a weird day."

"Yeah, it kind of has. And we're going to top it off by going all *Mission: Impossible*..."

"It'll be OK."

"And if it isn't? Why should you get the heat as well as me?"

"Look –" Stella squeezed Gabe's hand again, then let go – "if it looks at all like there's *any* chance we might get caught, we'll bail, OK?"

Gabe stared across the restaurant at the world outside, the early-evening traffic flowing by the windows. Benny and the old man were out there, and he couldn't help imagining them as roaming like a couple of hunting packs, him and Stella the prey. But they couldn't stay and eat pizza forever and if they were going to leave it might as well be to actually *do* something positive. Not hide like mice from a cat. Or an owl.

"OK."

For no good reason it had taken twice as long as the first time they'd done it to get the bike into Stella's car, but they'd finally tortured it into a shape that fit into the back of the Toyota and were on their way to Morrison High, Stella taking an off-the-main-drag route. Gabe was head down, fiddling around with the stereo, trying to find a station playing something decent, when Stella slammed on the brakes.

Gabe sat up. "Geez, Stella – what happened?"

Stella pulled over to the kerb. "I meant to ask you…"

"Ask me what?"

"The news … did you see it tonight?"

"No, why?"

"There was a report on the murder, at the antique store…"

"And?"

"There were two bodies…" Stella trailed off.

"Two?" Stella nodded. "Did they say who the other one was?"

"Apart from the owner, the guy you met, Cecil whatever, they figure the second one must've been

156

a customer. The reporter said it was, you know, unconfirmed, but he'd been told by a 'reliable source' –" Stella quote marked with her fingers – "that it looked like they'd both had their throats ripped out. By an animal."

Gabe stared at the digital read-out on the stereo, thinking, yeah, an animal all right; a coyote, had to be. And the second man, that was the person Cecil LeBarron had called, the client. Also had to be. He must have gone over to pick up the bracelet, and *so* been in the wrong place at the wrong time.

Gabe, not realizing what he was doing, reached up and touched the crucifix. "Let's get going, I *really* need this over with."

Chapter Twenty-One

Stella parked in the shadow of a tree overhanging the street that ran down one side of the school, sat back and looked at Gabe. "So?"

"What?"

"Exactly." Stella glanced out of the car, towards the high fence marking the extent of Morrison's grounds. "What next?"

"OK –" Gabe released his seat belt and reached for the door handle – "what's next is you stay here in the car and wait for me. I won't be long."

"So now I'm what, just the cab driver here?"

"I've been thinking…" Gabe opened the door, the courtesy light coming on; Stella's lips were a thin, straight line, her eyes slightly narrowed. "Look, OK … anything goes wrong, Stella, and I get caught? There's no need for *two* of us to get carpeted for this. Right?"

"Wrong." Stella grabbed the ignition key and her

bag and opened her door. "I told you I was coming, and like I said, you're only doing this because I took you to see Father Simon."

Gabe shrugged as he got out of the Toyota. There was obviously no point in arguing, so best get the show on the road as quickly as possible. He shut his door and stood looking up and down the street. He'd chosen this place as it was quiet and there weren't so many street lamps, but since the break-ins the school was now also protected by some rent-a-cop company – at least, they had put up signs saying they were.

"We'd better keep an eye out, OK?" Gabe said. Thinking to himself, *Yeah, we really had, what with real cops, Benny and a guy in a red baseball cap to think about as well.*

Stella nodded. "What happens now?"

"We get ourselves over the fence, get into the school, and we don't get caught. By anyone."

"Amen to that," Stella said.

Gabe spotted what he was looking for. "This way…"

Gabe had been on night walks in the school grounds a couple of times before as a dare, and it had gone like a breeze. Now that Stella was with him, though, he was doubly on edge walking though the grounds in the pitch dark, every tiny noise a potential threat. But they made it and reached the annexe with the supposedly hinky window without any trouble. As far as he remembered, it was a part of the school admin block, or maybe it was a storage facility. It wasn't somewhere students ever went, but it was connected directly to the main building.

"Keep your eyes and ears peeled, OK?" Gabe whispered, getting out the screwdriver he'd brought with him from his backpack and moving down to the first set of three windows, all of which were shut tight, as were the next ones.

"You sure this is the right place, Gabe?" Stella whispered from where she was keeping watch.

Gabe nodded. A lot of the buildings on the school grounds looked alike, but he thought he had the right one. This was not the time to look unsure of himself. Moving along until he was standing opposite the last window, he gave the wooden frame a sharp tug.

It gave, and a bit more than slightly. This was it. If he'd been sold a bill of goods then alarms would start going off and they would have to get out – and quick.

Nothing happened.

"Is this the one?"

Gabe jumped as Stella came up beside him. "Uh, yeah … yeah, looks like it…" He ran the shaft of the screwdriver up the narrow gap until he came to the loosened catch and then pushed. He'd expected it to flip up, but it didn't. Every minute they were left standing out in the open was a minute too long, in his opinion, and he pushed up even harder, wishing he'd thought to bring a hammer with him. Hell, the whole toolbox…

"Anything I can do, Gabe?"

"Not unless you happen to have a hammer with you…" Gabe placed the business end of the screwdriver on the latch and jabbed the base of the handle hard with the flat of his palm.

Once, nothing.

Twice, a slight movement.

The third time, his palm really hurting now, the catch gave and the screwdriver flew out of his

161

hand, clattering on to the concrete pathway. Gabe froze.

"It's OK," Stella whispered, picking up the screwdriver. "No one's here…"

Gabe gingerly pulled open the window; his armpits were prickling and he was hyped from the tension and they hadn't even really started yet. Gripping the sill with both hands he took a deep breath. "Nothing ventured, right?" he said as he hauled himself up.

Gabe slipped through the door into the main building, followed by Stella, and started running down the unlit corridor that went front to rear straight through the centre of the structure. The slap of their footsteps echoed off the walls, so loud he felt sure the noise could be heard out on the street. Gabe zigged left at the first turn, sneakers squealing like piglets as he took the corner, thirty metres down zagging right, finally coming to a halt midway down a wall of lockers. He dug into his jeans pocket, bringing out a key ring on the chain he had attached to a belt loop. Finding the right key, he opened the oversized, heavy-duty brass padlock on his locker, unhooked it and flipped open the clasp.

"What else are you stashing in there?" Stella pointed at the padlock.

"Nothing." Gabe swung the door back, reached in and felt around at the back of the locker for the package. "My dad gave it me when I started here, kind of a joke." He tried to ignore the tingling sensation he got when he touched the cloth. Tried to ignore the idea that the gold pieces were somehow aware of his presence.

"Is it there…? Have you got it?"

Something in Stella's voice made Gabe stop, package in hand, and look up at her. "What's the matter?"

"Thought I heard something…"

Gabe stuffed the gold in his backpack and refastened the padlock. "I've been thinking that ever since we came over the fence."

"We should go."

"I wasn't thinking of stay—"

Before he could finish, Stella took off at a sprint and he had his work cut out to catch up with her.

"Wait a second!" Gabe grabbed her arm as they

were about to turn the first corner. "What are we running from?"

Behind them, headlights raked through the front double doors like the spotlight on a prison tower and they both ducked down.

"That."

"Geez, are you psychic or something?"

Stella shook her head as they slipped down the corridor that led to the annexe. "Who knows, I just thought I heard something…"

In the distance car doors were being slammed, one after the other. As if life wasn't complex enough, he did not need to add 'fugitive from the law' to his list of problems.

They reached the room with the open window and Gabe nodded for Stella to get out first. While she made her exit, he waited by the door, listening for any clues as to what might be happening out the front of the building. He saw torch beams randomly stabbing into the darkened corridor and heard the front doors being rattled.

"Come on!"

Gabe looked round and saw Stella beckoning him from outside. He shut the door and was about to make for the window when he turned back and pressed in the lock mechanism on the handle.

"Gabe!"

"I'm there…"

"Hurry, before they come checking round the whole building."

As soon as he was out, Gabe reached for the screwdriver that should have been in his back pocket, but wasn't.

"Here." Stella gave it to him. "I picked it up when you dropped it."

"Right, thanks…" Gabe used the shaft to hold the catch up as he closed the window before letting it drop down. The second it had they both ran at full pelt, only stopping when they reached the tree by the fence that they'd used to get in.

Just as Gabe was about to give Stella a boost up, a sedan, tricked out to look like an actual cop car, came down the street. It was being driven slow, the occupants obviously ticking all the security company boxes by doing a final check round the school property. They both dropped to the ground until it had gone past.

"Close." Gabe stuck his head up and peered

down the street. Seeing the rent-a-cops had gone, he stood up. "All I gotta do is unclench my buttcheeks, but we did get away with it."

Stella grinned at him. "Father Simon, here we come."

Chapter Twenty-Two

Gabe took the folded duster out of his backpack and put it on the table in front of him. Father Simon, sitting in his armchair with a mug of coffee in one hand and an Oreo in the other, took a sip from the cup, then a bite of the cookie.

"I don't condone for one moment what you did, the two of you −" the Father shot them a mildly disapproving glance − "and you are more than lucky not to have been caught. That said, I fully understand why you did it, so let's see what you have, Gabe."

Gabe leant forward and unknotted the cloth, opening one corner at a time. In the middle of the frayed, faded yellow square sat the rest of the gold pieces he'd taken from the skeleton. Father Simon finished off his cookie in one bite, put down his mug and reached straight for the twisted and deformed crucifix.

"A terrible thing…" Father Simon turned the cross over and then back again, and looked closely at the second hole in its base. There was such a sadness in his eyes Gabe half expected he might be about to cry. "Apostasy at its worst and most dangerous. Faith lost and its power turned to evil… I've read about this, but never thought to see it, hold it in my own hands."

Gabe didn't want anything the Father was saying to be true, but the very first time he'd set eyes on the man in the red cap he had sensed there was something not right about him. And that was before anything bad had happened. Now just the thought of him sent chills down his spine and made his skin crawl. He realized that until he'd met this man he'd never really thought much about good and evil. But evil had his scent. It was after him.

"Who was he?" Gabe asked.

Father Simon looked up. "The man who owned this?" He held up the crucifix.

"Yeah." Gabe nodded.

Father Simon put down the cross on the table and reached to pick something up from the floor next to his chair. It was an old book, the leather binding on its spine and corners was cracked and worn, the thick pages rough-edged and yellowing. Carefully opening the book to where a marker had been placed, about a third of the way in, Father Simon turned it round so Gabe could see.

"I found this," he said, gently lifting the thin, translucent piece of paper that covered the colour picture on the left-hand page and holding it back.

Gabe could see the picture, which was about ten centimetres wide and eight centimetres high. It hadn't been printed on the actual page, but was a separate piece of paper glued in place. He looked at the very old-fashioned portrait of a man with a beard and the top of his head shaved bald, wearing the flowing robes of a monk. In his left hand the man held a skull, in the other what could only be a heart, blood dripping from it. Round his neck was a cross, which was hanging upside down.

"I did some digging around. Something I do rather well, even though I say so myself." Father Simon smiled slightly as he tapped the open book on his lap. "Having at one time been on the Index, though, this book took some finding."

"The Index?" Gabe looked at Stella, who shook her head.

"It's a book that listed *other* books which had been banned by the Church for being heretical, or anti-clerical. This one was deemed both," Father Simon said. "It's an old translation of an even older volume called *Liber Absentis* – the Book of Missing People, loosely put. It's a record of people, mostly priests, who strayed off the path of Truth and Light, and what their sins were."

"And you think that's the man who gave me the note?" Gabe leant forward to get a closer look at the portrait. "What's his name?"

"I can't be one *hundred* per cent sure, because there's something very strange about his story –" Father Simon shrugged – "but I think his name is Father Rafael Delacruz…"

"So he was a priest?"

Father Simon nodded. "The first time I found a mention of him is in the mid 1500s, the early days of the Spanish arrival in South America. Nothing unusual in that – if you remember, I told you about The Twelve Apostles of Mexico? He came over not long after they arrived, to help convert everyone the soldiers conquered. But in the *Liber Absentis* it says he died here, in what was then called Alta California,

probably in 1769. Over two hundred years later."
Father Simon closed the book. "As I said, a very
strange story, although I'm beginning to think that's
probably an understatement."

"Couldn't someone just have got the dates
wrong?" Gabe frowned. "You know, like a typo?"

"Always possible. Just because it's in print doesn't
mean it's right... I thought that, when I first saw
the inconsistency, but then I remembered the gold
objects you'd found. Particularly the knife."

Gabe looked at the ceremonial blade on the table.
It was the same as the one he'd seen cut out the
hearts of the two boys in his dreams.

"Look closer." Father Simon pointed at the
priest's left hand in the picture. "Behind the skull, see
anything?"

"Oh..." Stella put her hand up to her mouth.

"Geez ... it's the knife, right?"

"Maybe –" Father Simon picked up the sacrificial
knife – "or maybe just one very like it."

"This man, this Rafael ... how come he lived so
long?" Gabe stared out into the garden as he spoke.
"I mean that's like, I don't know, a vampire or
something. Was he a vampire? He couldn't be, right?"

"No… No, he couldn't." Father Simon closed the book. "Vampires don't exist, never have, but Father Rafael Delacruz did. According to what I've read, he started a cult, a kind of evil mix of powerful beliefs, cultures and sacred ceremonies, which involved blood sacrifice and soul slavery.

"Rafael was what we would describe today as a charismatic, a person who claims divine inspiration. These people wield immense influence on their followers, influence which grows with their ego. He was a dangerous man who, in 1574, escaped the clutches of the Church before they could deal with him. He went underground, disappeared with a small group of followers in the Sierra Madre mountains. He was never seen again."

"Until over two hundred years later?"

"That's right, Gabe, until over two hundred years later, and some nine hundred miles north." Father Simon opened the book again, turned a few pages and then ran his finger down, stopping at a specific paragraph. "It says here that his reappearance in this area coincided with a number of killings. Children having their hearts torn out while they were still alive.

"At first local native tribes, who didn't like the newcomers, were blamed. Then rumours spread of a man referred to by the Spanish as *Rey de los Infiernos*, King of the Underworld. The belief was that this man had the power to take over souls, and the more souls he gathered, the more powerful he became."

Gabe felt like he was looking at some kind of horrific virtual jigsaw puzzle, where the pieces kept remorselessly dropping into place. Everything fitted, and the picture was not a pretty one. "What happened to this Rafael?"

"No one knows, although once again it was believed he evaded capture by the Church." Father Simon steepled his fingers and was silent for a moment. "But I'd hazard a guess that they found him, eventually, and they killed him."

"You mean like the Inquisition?" Gabe said.

"Exactly like the Inquisition."

"And you think they buried him in that canyon?"

"Where they thought he'd never be found."

"Hard to think that these beautiful things belonged to such a terrible person." Stella picked up a ring and looked at it.

Gabe glanced down at the table and froze. He saw the crucifix, counted three rings, their red and blue stones glowing in the light, a bracelet, the knife and … where was the little, coin-sized thing? It wasn't there, but it couldn't *not* be there! Had he dropped it somewhere…? Was it still in his locker? He grabbed his backpack, frantically pulling everything out and searching its pockets. Nothing.

"What's the matter, Gabe?"

Gabe looked up at Stella. "There's a piece of the gold missing."

"Are you—?"

"I am *totally* sure, there was a small kind of medallion thing –" he held his thumb and forefinger apart a centimetre or so – "and now it's gone."

"Think, Gabe…" Father Simon's voice was calm, soothing. "Where did you last see it?"

"In my bedroom…" A picture flashed into Gabe's head: Remy walking towards him as he went back to his room after breakfast yesterday. It hadn't clicked then that there was only one place she could have come from because he'd been in a hurry, late for school, but it *had* to be her… She'd gone back to take a look at the secret things, all wrapped up on

174

his bedside table. Which he'd told her was none of her business. Red rag to a bull with his sister; Remy hated secrets.

"Gabe?" Stella touched his arm.

"My sister, Remy... My sister's got it."

Chapter Twenty-Three

"You don't know for *sure* she took it, Gabe..." Stella accelerated away the second the lights turned green and drove as fast as she dared; the last thing they needed was for a cop to pull her over for speeding.

"No ... no, I don't. Not for sure." Gabe had never felt so tense and frustrated in his whole life. "But I know my sister, and she is just *so* goddam *nosy*... I should've known... Oh God, what've I done?"

"Nothing, Gabe." Stella slowed to a halt for a 'Stop' sign, then sped away. "You didn't know, you *couldn't* have known what she was going to do, *or* that the things you'd found were so dangerous. How could you?"

"It's the next left."

"Got it, thanks." Stella reached over and patted his arm.

Gabe found himself relaxing slightly at her touch. Up ahead he saw his house, the family SUV parked out front, under the car port, lights on in the front room, everything looking completely normal. Stella pulled up on the driveway and they both leapt out, Gabe making straight for the side passage. He slammed the gate open and tore down to the kitchen door, Stella only a few steps behind him. Skidding to a halt, Gabe hesitated for a moment, then grabbed the handle and burst into the kitchen. It was empty, the rest of the house as silent as a stopped clock. For a couple of seconds Gabe didn't move, then Stella pointed at the sink.

"Gabe ... what's that?"

Drops of something, something dark, spattered on the pale cream tile of the work surface. And, now he looked, on the floor too. He moved closer, needing to get a better look but not wanting to, scared at what he might find, and saw there was a knife in the sink. There was blood on its ten-centimetre-long serrated blade.

"Mom! Dad!" Horrific slasher-vid images flickered in his head. Remy, poor little nosy Remy ripped to pieces by coyotes, gouts of blood splashed all down her T-shirt, the old man smiling, his teeth and face with blood on them, Remy's blood.

He ran for the door, which opened before he got there, his mom looking a mixture of puzzled and annoyed; she appeared to be fine, not a drop of blood anywhere on her. "Gabe, what on Earth's the matter?"

"Mom, the blood... Where's Remy? What's happened to her?"

"Remy? Nothing's happened, she's at Janna's, for a sleepover." Gabe's mom saw Stella and she smiled fleetingly in acknowledgement and looked back at her distraught son. "What's going on, Gabe, why would you think the blood was anything to do with Remy? Your father cut his hand slicing a bagel, I was just dealing with it."

"What? Janna's? She's at *Janna*'s?" The look on Gabe's face was so intense you could almost see the question marks hanging over his head. "When did she go? That's only a couple of blocks away ... Saloma Avenue. OK, OK – look, I can't explain right now, Mom. I can't... I have to go." He glanced at Stella. "We have to go..."

"What's going on, Gabe? I've never seen you like this..." Gabe's mom, fraught now, turned to Stella.

"Has he taken something, did *you* give it to him?"

"No, Mrs Mason! No, I didn't … he hasn't." Stella shook her head. "It's nothing like that, honest."

"Gotta go, Mom." Gabe grabbed Stella's hand and ran.

Halfway back to the car, Stella tried to slow him down. "Wait a second – what if Remy left the medallion here, Gabe?"

"If she'd left it here, *he'd* be here. That's what he wants."

Stella stopped and stood her ground. "Remy might've left it behind, and that man mightn't have got here yet, Gabe. You don't know, you haven't looked."

"I know my sister. Believe me, she's got it with her. You stay and look if you want to, but I have to get to Janna's…"

"OK, you're right." Stella ran to the driver's side of her car. "Let's go…"

As they drove away, Gabe's phone picked up a call, his mom's ringtone. He didn't want to take it, but the look on his mom's face as he'd left the kitchen made him realize he had to tell her something. He accepted the call.

"Yeah, Mom, look, it's OK… No, I'm not high or anything like that, really. OK? No, no, I didn't do anything… You're just gonna have to trust me… Call the cops?" He looked at Stella, making an '*I* don't know face'. She made a similar one back. "No, Mom, don't do that… I'll explain later." Gabe cut the call and slumped back in his seat. "This *has* to be a nightmare. Any minute now I am going to wake up. It can't be happening."

"I *really* wish…" Stella slowed as they approached a junction.

"Straight across, and I think it's the next right turn."

And then there it was, Saloma Avenue, Remy's best-friend-forever Janna's house a couple of hundred metres down on the right. Gabe had walked her there any number of times. And now they were getting close he didn't know what to do. He couldn't go storming in, like he had done at home, like he wanted to…

"Which house?"

Gabe focused in on the street. "There –" he pointed out of the car – "the blue plastic mailbox."

As Stella pulled over to the kerb, Gabe's heart sank. It looked as if the front door was ajar, a

180

narrow 'V' of light spilling out on to the front porch. That would not ordinarily have been such a bad thing. But tonight? Tonight he knew exactly what the phrase 'blood ran cold' meant. But Remy was in there. He had to get her out and he couldn't do that sitting in the car.

"OK…" Gabe's left hand automatically reached up for the cross around his neck as he opened the car door.

The two of them ran up the porch steps, both stopping at the front door; the wood around the lock was splintered. Voices were coming from inside, then a blare of music. Gabe wanted to yell out for his sister, but fear of what he might find stuck the words in his throat, choking him. He dry swallowed as he pushed the door open further, took a hold of himself and walked into the house.

Like the kitchen back at home, the front room at Janna's was also empty, but with signs that people had recently been there, and left in a hurry. The TV was on, playing an ad for some gross double-size bacon-cheese-and-everything burger. On the oval coffee table, set in front of a big, open fireplace, there were soda bottles, one on its side still dribbling its dark brown contents on to the carpet; half-empty plastic glasses, candy and snack food scattered everywhere. Looked like a food fight had started, but where were the sleepover girls?

Where the heck was Remy?

Gabe was trying to make some kind of sense of what he was seeing when, in a sliver of silence between ads, other voices could be heard. Muffled, raised voices from somewhere else in the house. The hairs on the back of Gabe's neck stood to attention and his scalp prickled. He shot a glance at Stella and made a dash across the room for the door that led to the rest of the single-storey house.

"Remy!" Gabe hauled the door open.

Down at the end of the wide hallway, his back to him, stood a figure in faded jeans, a brown leather coat and a red baseball cap. If Father Simon was right, a reborn, resurrected Rafael Delacruz. And at his side, hackles up, ears flat back, stood a slim, grey coyote. Which probably meant there was another one around somewhere. Gabe stopped, checked behind him – no coyote – and looked back down the corridor. The double doors to the large master bedroom at the rear of the house were closed and behind them Gabe could hear the girls crying and shouting.

With just a cross hanging round his neck, Stella there beside him, the last thing Gabe felt like was the cavalry, riding in to the rescue. More like the Lone Ranger. But his sister was in real danger and here he was. What he should do next he hadn't quite figured out, except that doing nothing was not an option.

Chapter Twenty-Four

The figure at the end of the corridor made the first move. He turned round, slowly, and even at a distance Gabe could immediately see there was a difference, something strange about the man he now understood to be this Rafael. His face looked younger, and he seemed to be standing up straighter, the shoulders of his jacket filled out better.

Was that a trick of the light...? Was he also imagining the deep red glow in the man's eyes? The worms of an old, old fear of the peculiar and the unknown awoke in the pit of Gabe's stomach, squirmed into life and began eating into him.

He could feel Stella's breath on his neck she was standing so close. She'd tensed up as this person, he couldn't be called 'old' any more, had turned round. She gasped, shocked, the moment she saw his face, gripping Gabe's arm tight as if she'd fall over if she let go. Gabe wanted to tell her it was all going to be

OK, but that would be a lie and they'd both know it.

"You gotta go, Stella." Jaws clenched, Gabe edged backwards. "Get out, now…"

Rafael, the coyote at his side, was coming towards them, walking head held up now. Proud. He was flexing his fingers, and then he splayed them and held his arms out wide in front of him, just like he was coming to embrace Gabe and Stella. Except, like the coyote, he was snarling and the look on his face was anything but warm or welcoming.

"Go, Stella…"

"No. I know you won't leave without Remy … and I'm not leaving without you."

Under any other circumstances Gabe would have been kind of flattered by that statement. Watching the man with a murderous fire in his eyes coming towards them, he just felt the weight of extra responsibility land like a vulture on his shoulder, panic slithering up from his gut, trying to take control. An emotional pincer movement.

And the closer Rafael came, the worse it got.

He and the coyote were now over halfway up the hallway, and Gabe could feel the air around him crackling with static electricity. Fear made real.

He couldn't stop his synapses sparking, like crazed firecrackers going off, jumping here and there, from one random, idiot idea to another. All he'd done so far was move back into the TV room, which wasn't even a half decent Plan B.

The knowledge gained from all the years of reading comic books and watching action movies said that what he *really* needed was some kind of kick-ass weapon. A rocket-propelled grenade, maybe a flamethrower, either would be great, they really would. He'd never even held a pistol, let alone anything bigger, but right now he could *really* do with some leverage – that was for pretty damn sure.

And then, with no warning, the banshee wailing came s-c-r-e-a-m-i-n-g back into Gabe's head.

The jolt was much greater than it had been in the canyon. The sound louder. Higher-pitched. Sharper, like red-hot needles jabbing in his brain. Again and again and again. Somewhere a small part of him realized that the strangled screaming was coming from him, and the warm, sticky fluid he felt on his hands, that was his too. Father Simon had known he was going to die, and here he was, about to go into the final fade.

Stella, who had been sticking to him like they were Velcroed together, staggered away as she saw Gabe, face contorted and gargoyled, bent double, hands to his ears, blood leaking through his fingers.

It was the sight of her horrified, wide-eyed expression that snapped something inside Gabe and gave him access to a core strength he never knew he possessed. This Rafael, this dead-priest-walking, wherever he came from and however he'd got here, was not simply going to trample all over him like he was no more than dirt on the ground, and then discard his lifeless husk.

Not going to happen.

Chapter Twenty-Five

Summoning up what felt like an almost superhuman degree of control, Gabe forced himself to ignore the pain, push it away and stand straight, legs apart. It was the hardest thing he'd ever done. Hands clenched tight, the outward expression of the huge effort he was making to stop himself from falling apart, he stared back at Rafael, looked straight into the heat of his dark, burning eyes.

Father Simon believed *he*, Gabriel Mason, had somehow brought this evil back to life, dragged it here from whatever hell it had been sent to centuries ago.

Father Simon believed he'd *prayed* and his prayers had been answered in the shape of the thing now just a few metres away from him. And Gabe had, for a moment, believed it could be true, got sucked right into Father Simon's story.

But it wasn't *his* story.

He could see now how it had to be. Wavering

like a candle near an open window, the dim light of revelation illuminated the truth. He had to believe in his own story or he was lost. Gone.

Instead of giving in, Gabe did the opposite and went on the attack.

"I don't believe in you, in *any* of this!" Gabe fumbled inside his T-shirt and grabbed at the cross, yanking it so hard it felt like a red-hot knife slicing across the back of his neck.

He held up his fist, defiant, the cross dangling from its broken chain, and threw it at Rafael. The intricate tangle of fine gold links and the cross they were attached to seemed to float through the air between them. A twisting, snake-like arc of precious metal and symbolism. Gabe followed after it, fists flying. All the pent-up anger that he'd kept tamped down for days now rose up to the surface and boiled over. He'd been scared for far too long. It wasn't his fault that he'd stumbled on the skeleton, found the gold and taken it to help his family out of some bad times!

Not! His! Fault!

Gabe punched Rafael's stunned face. He could feel his knuckles as they hit bone, saw the astonishment in those coal-dark eyes, watched blood drops fly lazily from the man's mouth. Every punch hurt Gabe too, sent shockwaves of pain buzz-sawing through him, but he couldn't stop. He would die before he stopped. This close to the man the air around them became feverishly, suffocatingly hot, the smell of old earth overpowering, but through it all there was just one thought ringing, clear as a bell in Gabe's head. Kill him!

In between punches Gabe saw Rafael's look of surprise and disbelief change, and figured he was about to begin fighting back. Gabe was expecting to have to fend off a rain of iron-fisted jabs, which didn't come. Instead his opponent dismissively pushed him away, then stepped back and pointed at him.

"It doesn't ... matter to me ... what you believe..." Rafael's chest was heaving, his words punctuated by deep, rattling breaths, making him sound so very old. *"We ... are ... connected, acolyte..."*

Gabe stood, unsteady on his feet, puzzled. Why wasn't Rafael fighting? What was he saying? What did he mean, *connected*?

"No." Gabe shook his head, tiredness soaking through him. "No, we're not."

"Denial is pointless ... you came to me, you found me

190

… you do believe and you are the first of so many more …
the first disciple!"

"No…" The voice was in Gabe's head. Again. He hadn't realized at first, but Rafael's lips weren't moving. The man was right, denial was pointless. There was a connection. And he had made it possible, he had allowed this wicked, corrupt monster to breathe again. To breathe and become more and more powerful with every breath.

"Gabe?"

Gabe glanced to his right, shocked to see Stella brandishing a wrought-iron poker in both hands… The second coyote had made an appearance and Stella was making like Xena and fending off both of them with the poker.

"Gabe, what's happening? Why are you just standing there, *looking* at him?"

"*You cannot break this.*" In front of him Rafael smiled, eyes hooded, his top lip curled back. "*Bring me what is mine. All of it. I have work to complete, a mission to accomplish!*"

The next chunk of time – minutes, possibly a lot of minutes, Gabe had no idea how many – went by in a total blur.

Rafael was there when he turned towards Stella and the coyotes, and he had disappeared when he looked back. In his place, Stella was now standing in front of him, frowning, concerned. She shook him gently, then she too was gone, between one blink and the next, only to return with a damp cloth, which she started wiping his face and hands with.

The room filled with all kinds of people, some he recognized, like Janna's parents, most he didn't. It was chaotic, everyone talking at the same time, some crying, a few shouting, some in uniform, quite a number of them talking directly to him. At him. Gabe didn't even try to make sense of what was going on. There were handshakes, and for some reason he couldn't fathom, pats on the back. But Remy was there; little nosy Remy was hugging him, crying then not crying. There, alive and unhurt, with her pink Hello Kitty backpack, clutching his hand. And then they were walking down the driveway with Stella. Stella holding Remy's other hand. He was with Remy in the back of the car, still gripping the crucifix and broken chain, then putting it in his pocket. Stella driving away from Janna's house. And as she drove, the further down the road they got, it felt like the world finally came back into focus, sound synched with vision. Tuned in.

"You were brave, Gabey." Remy leant in close. "Everyone said."

"I don't know about that." Gabe gave his sister a hug.

"You were," Stella glanced back. "Believe me."

"Remy?" Gabe tried to sound as nonchalant as he could. "That little thing you borrowed from my room, yeah?"

Remy, who could spot trouble coming a mile off, moved away from her brother slightly. "You had so much, and it was the littlest, Gabey, so I didn't think you'd notice… And I only *borrowed* it, honest."

Gabe held out his hand. Remy dug into the front pocket of her pink Hello Kitty backpack and gave him the medallion.

"Sorry, Gabey…"

"It's OK." Gabe squeezed Remy's shoulder. But no way was it OK, no way at all.

There was a tap on his bedroom door, which Gabe knew would be his dad. He'd figured he wouldn't be able to get away without some kind of confrontation about what had happened at Janna's, and he supposed now was as good a time as any to have it. He had a story which, as Remy was asleep, no one would be able to check on straight away, so there was nothing left to do but get it over with.

"Yeah?"

The door opened and his dad came in, this time walking straight over and pulling up the ratty office chair Gabe had salvaged off the street a couple of years ago.

"OK … you kind of freaked your mother out, earlier on." His dad sat back, the old chair creaking. "You and Sarah rushing out of the house like that, no explanation."

"Stella."

"Sorry, Stella. And I know everything worked out fine, Gabe, but what *I* don't understand is how *you* knew there was anything going on at Janna's in the first place?" His dad made a 'beats me' face.

"It was a hunch."

"A hunch?"

"Yeah…" Gabe shrugged, hoping he looked way more relaxed than he felt. "Like, there's been some guy hanging round and I was, you know, worried?"

Gabe's eyes flicked from his dad to his laptop screen and back. He was going to have to take a risk now, and hope it worked out.

"Remy saw him too."

His dad stiffened. "Did you tell the cops this?"

"I guess so…" Gabe rubbed his eyes with his knuckles and shook his head. "I guess I did, I don't remember. It's all, you know, kind of like a blur? What I did and what I said?"

"Sure, I understand." Gabe's dad reached over and patted his knee. "A bit of a shock, right?"

Too right, Gabe thought, smiling lamely and nodding.

His dad got up. "You did good, Gabe, real good… You must be tired."

"Yeah…" No argument there.

"End of the day, all that matters is that you're both fine." His dad went to the door. "Crazy world out there… See you tomorrow, OK?"

"Sure, dad," Gabe said, thinking, *You have no idea…*

Chapter Twenty-Six

Gabe looked back at his house, then walked over to the Toyota where Stella was waiting for him. He felt exhausted, but no surprises there as he hadn't slept that well, and he'd had to get up earlier than he'd wanted so that he could have time to talk to Remy before Stella came. If she was asked, Remy had promised – cross her heart and hope to die – to say she'd seen a strange man, and that she'd told him about it. In return, Gabe had had to swear to be nice to her forever, and buy her a present. His little sister drove a hard bargain.

"Thanks for doing this, Stella." Gabe felt back for his seat belt, found it and put it on. "I cannot believe last night, and I can*not* believe you are here, driving my sorry bones around, my bike still in the back of your car. Sorry about that... Sorry about everything."

"A girl's gotta do." Stella started the car. "You

have to get that medallion to Father Simon, and this is the quickest way it's going to get done."

"After everything you saw? I figured you'd drop me and Remy off and that'd be the last I'd ever see of you. Really." As Stella drove away from his house Gabe leant forward. He stared at the dashboard and massaged his temples while he talked. "I mean the whole school thing – breaking in? That was big, but it was *kinder*garten compared to what happened at Janna's. *I* don't even remember a half of what went on there, which, considering what I do remember, is probably a good thing."

He glanced at Stella. "I mean, really? I was sure there was no way I was gonna get off this thing lightly, but all I got was my dad wondering how I knew something was going on at Janna's."

"What did you tell him?"

"Made some shit up about seeing some guy hanging round."

"He bought it?"

"Uh-huh," Gabe nodded.

Stella slowed to a halt at a junction. "Do you always go to such lengths to make yourself seem interesting on a first date?"

Gabe looked at her, amazed. *First date?*

"I gotta say –" Stella turned right – "you *really* freaked me out, the way you looked when that guy – what did Father Simon say his name was?"

"Rafael."

"Right… When he came into the room with the, you know…"

"Coyote?"

"Yeah. Teeth on legs. I thought you were going to, I don't know what I thought… It was like you'd gone *totally* catatonic? But you were amazing, especially when the cops came to Janna's house. No panic, just went with the flow, didn't say too much of anything and let people make their own minds up about what'd gone down. Genius. Let them have it whichever way they want, whatever way makes sense to them."

"What did you say when they asked you about what happened?"

"Nothing. Acted all girly, cried a bit and took care of Remy. They left me alone."

"OK…" Gabe smiled.

"I can do 'all girly' when I need to!" Stella punched Gabe's arm lightly. "And now *you* have to tell me, now there's just the two of us, what was going on with you and that weirdo? The bleeding, and your face? I mean you looked like you were screaming, but no noise – and all the intense staring, after you'd been trying to bust each other's faces apart? Man, that was *so* bizarre."

Gabe quit looking at Stella and stared out of the car window. Bizarre wasn't the half of it; he figured the only reason he hadn't been hauled off to a Psych Ward somewhere was that he didn't have the energy to have a meltdown. But what was he supposed to tell her? The truth? Oh right. *That* was going to see him get a second date.

"Just tell me, Gabe. How bad can it be?"

Gabe glanced at Stella and then looked out of the window again. "Oh, I don't know, pretty bad."

"Come on, no secrets."

"I'm hungry, you know?"

"Don't change the subject."

"I can't be totally honest on an empty stomach, and I mostly skipped breakfast."

Stella pointed at the dash. "Emergency peanut M&M's stash is in the glove compartment."

"Cool." Gabe opened the packet, lodged it in

the central console and took a handful. This was it. "So, the thing of it is, I can hear him, that guy Rafael? I can hear him in my head, Stella. Right *inside* my head. He talks to me. And I can, you know ... talk to him. He told me we were connected. And the creepiest thing? D'you remember how I described him?"

Gabe could see the expression on Stella's face change.

"Yeah, I do... You said he was an old guy."

"Right, and now he's a *lot* younger than the first time I saw him."

In the silence that followed, Gabe's imagination ran around doing somersaults, constructing all the different ways Stella could/would/should react to what he'd said. None of them very positive.

"OK, right ... that is certifiably weird." Stella took some M&M's. "So did he say anything else?"

"You don't think any of this means I'm insane?"

"Yeah, sure, it sounds crazy, but if you say that's what happened, I believe you. I saw *some*thing going on between the two of you, and actually what you just told me is about as logical an explanation as anything else I can think of right now. Kinda fits with the rest of the scenario, right?"

Gabe took a handful more candy, wondering at this girl's ability to stay calm in the face of a crisis; OK, so it was his crisis, his head that had been invaded by The Insane Undead Creature from the Canyon, but still, there were no visible signs she was freaking out. "He said I couldn't break the connection, and that I had to give him back everything I'd taken. All of it, he said... Give him all of it."

"Don't think that sounds like such a great idea, somehow. Leastways, that was the vibe I was getting from Father Simon."

"But what's *he* gonna do with it? You know, the gold? Some sort of exorcism ceremony?"

"No idea."

"D'you think he'll have to do the same kind of thing with me, to break the connection with..." Gabe stifled a yawn, and blinked gritty eyes. "Sorry, I'm kinda blitzo..."

"Not surprised. I wonder why he just left..."

"Who?"

"What was his name? The man, Rafael... Why'd he just up and leave like that?"

"No idea..."

"One minute he looked like he could spit bricks, the next he just walked out the house."

Gabe remembered what this Rafael person had said. Something about how *he* had come to him… '*You came to me, you found me,*' that's what he'd said. And then the man had repeated that he had to return everything.

"Gabe?"

"Sorry … I was just, you know, thinking…"

"And?"

"And I think he didn't kill me because he needs me."

Chapter Twenty-Seven

After there'd been no reply to ringing the bell or knocking, Stella tried the door to the rectory.

"I don't think it's ever locked," she said, turning the handle. The door swung open with hardly a sound, revealing a dark, empty hallway leading down to the Father's study door at the end.

For the third time Gabe found himself about to enter what appeared to be an empty house. But maybe it meant nothing. Maybe the Father was already over at the church doing a service, what did he know? He stood on the threshold, the possibility he might have to face another round of ear-bleeding brain damage making him about ready to throw up. But he knew there was no way he could let Stella go in alone. They had to find out if Father Simon was all right.

"Father?" Stella walked into the hallway, reaching to her left and flicking on the hall lights. "Are you there?"

Swallowing hard, Gabe followed her inside and closed the door. The click of the latch seemed oddly loud in the eerie quiet of the house. They went down the hall, it felt in slo-mo, Gabe noting that the doors to each room they passed, two on either side, were shut. Which did not mean anything at all. He kept walking and as Stella reached for the study's door handle he beat her to it.

"I'll go first…"

Gabe stood in the doorway scanning the room, but there was no sign of Father Simon, dead or alive. The place looked exactly the way it had when he'd first walked in, just yesterday. The same, except for a number of open books on the Father's desk, and more of the same, plus a yellow legal pad, piled on the low table. Research, old-school, pre-Google style, Gabe thought, then saw there was a closed laptop among the books.

No body, no blood spatter, no Father Simon. And no sign of the gold pieces from the canyon.

"You thought I might, like, faint or something, Gabe?"

Stella came from behind Gabe and went over to the desk, where she started looking at the books.

"No, but he's your friend. I didn't want you to have to see what I thought might be here."

"Oh, OK…" Stella looked up and flashed him a smile. "Thank you."

Gabe walked round the settee to the table and picked up the legal tablet. There was some writing at the top of the page, a message a few lines long in pencil, and a ragged edge where the bottom third had been roughly torn off.

"There's a note, Stella."

"What? What does it say?"

"Guy shoulda been a doctor, his handwriting's so bad." Gabe squinted at the paper.

"Here, let me see." Stella took the pad, went over to the desk and turned on the lamp. "'Stella and Gabriel'," she read, holding the pad close to the light, "'I couldn't wait for you to come back here as there is something I've had to deal with as a matter of urgency. If you have brought the last piece with you, please leave it in the top right-hand drawer of my desk. Lock the drawer and take the key with you'."

"He went without us?"

"Looks like it —" Stella bent down closer to the pad

– "and it also looks like he might've written down the address of where he went – I need a pencil!"

"But the thing is, *when* did he go? For all we know it might've been last night." Gabe wandered over to the table to see if he could work out what the Father had been looking for in the books and saw a green light pulsing on the laptop's front edge. It hadn't been turned off, and an idea parachuted lazily into his head. Gabe sat down, flipped open the laptop and brought up Father Simon's browser. He was still using Safari, and the machine was old and slow, but finally Gabe accessed the browser's Recent History dropdown and smiled when he saw the last site the Father had gone to – a page on Wikipedia.

"Pretty sure he's gone to something called 'Mission San Sebastian de los Ángeles' –" Gabe double-clicked and brought the page up – "in Mission Hills."

"How…?" Stella looked up from trying to figure out what the Father had written by rubbing a pencil over the imprint left on the second page of the legal pad.

"Magic fingers." Gabe clicked and clicked again. A small all-in-one on top of a two-drawer filing cabinet next to the Father's desk chugged into life and started to print.

Chapter Twenty-Eight

"You, Gabriel my friend, are either deaf as I do not know what, or got *way* less smarts than I had you pegged for."

As Stella turned to go to her car, Gabe spun round awkwardly, like he was doing a dance move he hadn't practised nearly enough. Coming out of Father Simon's house, neither of them had noticed the pale grey van parked the other side of the street from the rectory. Benny, a lit cigarette stuck in the side of his mean little mouth, was rolling the half-open window the rest of the way down as he spoke.

"You think he's deaf or stupid, Nate?" Benny said, head on one side.

Looking over his shoulder, Gabe saw Nate Kansky, Benny's other go-to guy, standing by Stella's car. As Scotty was no doubt behind the wheel, the full bozo crew was out today.

"Musta got the brains of a hammer ain't got no head, my opinion."

"I think you have that right, Nate, nailed it in one." Benny got out of the van, took a drag and pointed at Gabe, the cigarette between his fingers. "I thought I had made myself, you know, clear, Gabriel. Told you to stay away from little Miss Grainger here? Right? Didn't I do that?"

Even if he'd been trying to imagine how a day could go downhill any quicker, Gabe was pretty sure it would have taken him some time to come up with this scenario.

"What are you—?"

"I'm not talking to you, missy," Benny cut Stella off. "Not yet anyways." He turned back to Gabe and held up the cigarette by its tip, like it was evidence in a trial. "See this? See what you have made me do? I was going *so* good, until you started acting stupid, Gabriel, not doing what you'd been told."

Benny flicked the cigarette at Gabe. It missed, sailing over his left shoulder.

"But I am gonna deal with you later –" Benny signalled to Nate – "as I have other business to attend to now."

208

Nate, left arm around Stella, had his right hand over her mouth. As he hustled her towards the van, Gabe grabbed at his shirt and tried to haul him back, stopping only when he saw the large gun that had appeared in Benny's hand.

"Later, Gabriel." Benny waved the barrel, a little up, a little down. "You hear me now? You feel me?"

Gabe nodded without even thinking, one eye on Stella, struggling hard as she was shoved into the rear of the van. Nate got in after her and slid the door shut. He kept his other eye on Benny and the gun. Benny who had no doubt been watching back-to-back gangsta movies, the way he was talking.

"Don't deal with her, deal with *me*, Benny!" Gabe shouted. He couldn't believe this was all going down on a nice suburban street, *and* outside a rectory. Where were all the curtain-twitching neighbours when you needed them? "This is all my fault, not hers."

"No fret, guy, you-all will have your turn." Benny smiled, spat and got back in the van. He leant out of the window. "As the cops like to say, 'Don't leave town'."

Gabe watched the Chevy van drive off down the street in total disbelief. How was it possible that

Benny had found them? Except somehow he had and now he'd got Stella. Gabe wanted to slap himself in the face – he'd let Benny take Stella, and done nothing to stop him! Apart from not get himself shot. He was worse than useless. And what was he going to do now, how was he going to get the medallion to Father Simon? Because they hadn't left it locked in the drawer, like he'd asked, they were on their way to... Gabe's jaw dropped.

The medallion was in Stella's bag! It'd be safer in there, she'd said...

Gabe's heart sank as the full, ghastly implication of what had just occurred slowly revealed itself.

Benny had Stella. Stella had the medallion, and the car keys. And he was left standing on the sidewalk, unable to do anything. On top of which, his bike was in the car. But even if it wasn't, what could he do? Chase after Benny on two wheels?

He paced up and down, cursing himself for not having been exposed to mega doses of gamma radiation, or whatever else you had to do to become a superhero and leap tall buildings, trash your enemies with your retractable metal claws and save the day. Which was when he saw something on the asphalt, glinting in the early-morning sunlight. He went over, bent down and picked up Stella's car keys. Had she dropped them by accident, or on purpose? He looked at the car. At least now he could get his bike. Or...

Gabe stood up. He didn't have a full driver's licence but he could drive, kind of. No, he could, he'd had a *lot* of time behind the wheel with his dad, practising in parking lots and side streets and suchlike. But his dad had lost his job and the project ground to a halt. He stared at the Toyota. If he was careful ... if he was lucky ... he could get away with it.

"But where?" Gabe whispered to himself, thunderclouds of frustration making it hard to think. If he did risk it, where was he going to drive to? It was like being a character in someone else's game, and he was being given things, but not told what to do with them. Did he go back to Stella's house, tell her parents what had happened to their daughter, and would they believe a word of what he said? Maybe the cops? Nope, that'd probably be the exact the same deal.

Gabe went over and unlocked the car.

Got in.

Closed the door.

Put the keys in the ignition.

Took a bunch of emergency M&M's, as this sure as hell was an emergency.

Ate six or seven chocolate-covered peanuts in one go and thought about starting the car.

He wanted more than anything to believe that Benny would not do anything bad. Very stupid? Yes. Possibly motivated by the last dumb movie or TV show he'd watched? Also yes. But not real, actual bad.

Just the thought that he might hurt Stella was driving him crazy, but as there was no way he could figure out where Benny had gone with her, there was no point in wasting time trying to follow a trail that didn't exist on a map he didn't have. None at all.

But he did have an idea where Father Simon might be: the Mission San Sebastian de los Ángeles in Mission Hills. The site of one of the early Spanish religious settlements in what was, as Father Simon had told them, then called Alta California and part of the Spanish Empire. According to the Wikipedia pages he'd printed out and skimmed.

And the only reason he could think of for Father Simon to go there was if he thought that was where he'd find Rafael Delacruz, the resurrected man. The evil person whom he believed Gabe had brought back to life. He *had* to have gone there, with the gold, for some kind of religious version of a Dodge City cowboy showdown. Crucifixes at dawn. It would be hilarious if he didn't have a recent and very personal experience of what the man the Father was up against was capable of.

Gabe started the car.

Chapter Twenty-Nine

The drive had been intense. Nothing remotely terrible happened, but he had spent the entire journey just waiting for the bad-luck axe to fall on him from a great height. Mainly because he couldn't stop repeating his dad's watchwords when he was giving him lessons. Just be careful and don't worry about *your* driving; instead, worry about what all the other idiots on the road are doing.

And boy, had he worried.

So much that his main concern became getting pulled over for being terminally cautious and driving too slow. By the time he arrived at the Mission, Gabe sincerely doubted he had any nerves left unshredded. He got out of the car and took a look round at where he was.

From the quick scan he'd given the Wikipedia article he knew that the original adobe structure had been badly damaged in a big quake in 1857, rebuilt and then added to over the years. The long, low-rise building, set some way back from the street with a broad, tree-dotted lawn sloping down towards him, was described by the article as 'something of an architectural mongrel'. This Sunday morning the Mission San Sebastian looked fine to him, odd only in that it was genuinely old, unlike just about everything else in LA. And it also looked like no one was there. No visitors he could see, no staff or whatever, the place all quiet and empty.

Crossing the road he couldn't stop himself from anxiously scanning here, there and everywhere to see if he was being watched. Like by a coyote, or an owl. He walked up to a small side gate, thinking he had to keep his wits about him and try to spot any trouble before it found him. The gate was unlocked and Gabe let himself through, mentally tossing a coin as to which way he should go. Right, along the terracotta-roofed walkway with its long line of flattened arches, or left, towards the taller, two-storey structure with a cross on the roof, aka the actual church part of the Mission. Instead of guessing, he got the folded sheets of paper out of his back pocket and referred to the small schematic of the grounds for any clues that might help make up his mind.

It looked like there was a smaller chapel behind the church, in an area marked 'Cemetery'. The caption said it was the oldest original building of the Mission. He couldn't call it logic – nothing that had happened to him over the last few days had been remotely logical – but it felt like if Rafael, the devil-worshipping returnee, had a connection to anywhere in this place it would be the most ancient part. The part that had been around when Rafael had last been here.

When he reached the far corner of the main church building, Gabe stopped, flattened himself against the wall and poked his head round for a quick recce, then felt kind of ridiculous. Why was he acting like he was Agent Gabriel Mason here? Because you never knew. Definitely a good enough reason, he told himself.

He looked again. There was nobody around in this part of the grounds, either, and not so far away Gabe could see the line of trees behind which was the graveyard. In there, if he was right and if he wasn't too late, he'd find Father Simon. *Dead or alive,* said the voice in his head.

Out in the surrounding area some animal or other uttered a strange, almost-human sound, halfway between a scream and a moan, and it made Gabe tense up. He'd been trying not to think about what might be happening to Stella, in the back of the van with Benny, Scotty and Nate. While it wasn't his fault she'd gotten under Benny's skin, he couldn't help feeling it was his fault Stella hadn't been safely at home today, where Benny couldn't get his hands on her.

But if he opened up the floodgates to the unending list of 'what if?' possibilities, he knew he'd be drowned by them and unable to think of anything else. Or actually do anything. He didn't want to stop himself worrying about Stella, but in this particular here and now he had to. He had to believe Benny wouldn't do anything terrible, while he knew for a fact that Rafael absolutely would. With a quick glance behind him, Gabe peeled himself off the church wall and ran for the trees.

He had spent so much time playing first-person shooter games he found it impossible not to imagine there really was a sniper up on the church roof, with him in the cross hairs of his telescopic, laser-guided sights. Every metre he covered, the trees that would give him sanctuary seemed to remain just as far away, only adding to his chances of being hit by the sniper's high-powered, hollow-point bullet. The bullet that would punch through his skin, its copper alloy jacket peeling apart, the lead core fragmenting on impact, then tearing up and making hamburger of his insides. He'd read all about it. He knew every single stage of what was going to happen, that he wouldn't even hear the kill shot.

And then there he was, running through the narrow stand of trees, moments later coming out the other side. Safe. Unscathed. In the graveyard.

Gabe stopped to get his breath back, as well as some of the sanity he'd lost in the previous twenty seconds. He scanned the area around him. There was no way a cemetery – even during the day, with a total lack of cold, silver moonlight – was not going to be spooky. The place was full of dead people, what else was it going to feel like? But in the silence, the only sound his own ragged breathing, there was the same zing of electricity in the air that there'd been earlier, at Janna's house. But this time it was more intense.

The man was here, somewhere. And he was getting stronger.

Out of the corner of his eye Gabe caught a brief flare of light over to his right, like someone had just taken a picture and the flash had gone off. In that direction he saw a small building, which, if he was reading the map right, had to be the old chapel. Although what he was going to do if he found Father Simon locked in mortal combat with Rafael, he hadn't got a clue. In his pocket he still had the crucifix, which Stella had picked up off the floor at Janna's and returned to him, but when it came to a weapon, that was about it.

A saying of his mom's, or maybe it was his grandma's, came back to him, about how the brave went where angels feared to tread. He was with the angels on this one – he did not feel brave and, if there'd been any other alternative, he would not be about to tread anywhere but back to the car.

Dodging between the ranks of graves of the long-dead, some abandoned to nature and with stones leaning at crazy, drunken angles, others neat and well tended, he saw the flashing light go off again, twice, three times. Coming from inside the chapel.

Whatever was happening it looked as if it was hotting up, just in time for his arrival. As he got closer, Gabe slowed down. He could see the place better now; the roof of the small building sagging like the back of an old horse, it looked every day of its two hundred and some years of age.

He arced round to the left, where the door had to be, keeping his distance until he was facing the front of the chapel. The double doors were open. As Gabe strained to see inside he heard the wing-whisper, then he saw the owl, a grey phantom, glide between him and the building. Reining back his fear, he searched the cemetery for the coyotes, finally spotting them, their fur the perfect camouflage against the gravestones. Sentry-like, they were sitting either side of the low building. They were warning him off.

Looking back at the chapel he caught a movement. He was going to have to ignore the coyotes. Inside, he could see the figure of a man... No, make that two men.

Chapter Thirty

When he got into big trouble as a child, Gabe remembered his mom asking him what had possessed him to do whatever it was he shouldn't have done. As if she wanted to believe it wasn't really his fault and he had no control over himself. Standing outside the chapel, the sensation of being taken over, possessed, spread out through his whole body from deep inside and invaded every part of him. More mist than smoke, as he breathed he could feel the coldness swallowing him up. And there was nothing he could do to stop its progress.

He began to move forward, not really knowing if he was being pulled unwillingly towards the chapel or walking steadfastly into whatever was going down in there of his own accord.

By the time he had stepped through the open doors it didn't much matter either way. He was inside, where the normal rules – the ones which made the world as he recognized it turn – did not apply any more. He knew this to be true because he'd been in the exact situation before. And only just survived.

In the small, confined space where he now found himself, the air was alive with a loud buzzing, like hornets on steroids, and thick with the acrid scent of burnt herbs and a hot, metallic smell he couldn't identify. The vile mixture clung to Gabe's nostrils, the taste coating his mouth, and it made his eyes water. He waited for the screaming and the jagged, agonizing knives to begin stabbing at him. Waited for his head to start expanding until his skull disintegrated from the pressure. But nothing happened.

Or maybe it just hadn't happened yet.

A couple of metres away Gabe saw Father Simon with his back to him; he was stock-still, hands held up and out to the side, his white hair a startled, frizzy crown on his head.

In contrast, some four or five metres further back, a red-eyed figure strode left and right, reminding Gabe of a caged animal obsessively pacing in a zoo. Behind him there was what could have been a low table with something on it, but Gabe couldn't make out what. Dusty sunlight reflected dully off the man's

222

dark, slicked-back hair. The red baseball cap might have gone, but it was the same person he'd last seen at Janna's.

Rafael looked so different Gabe's heart almost stopped there and then. He was much wilder than before and his barely contained anger seemed to give the man a rippling aura, as if he was sending out intense waves of heat, and every time he randomly punched the air there was a sharp burst of light. Then the man pointed straight at him.

"You came! My disciple, you *came*!"

This time the voice didn't echo in Gabe's head. He could hear it for real. See the man's eyes flare as he spoke.

"Yeah, I did!" The words, a dry croak, stuck in his throat and any moment he expected the attack to begin. "I came to help stop you!"

The man laughed, a harsh crow-like caw, and Father Simon swung round.

"Gabriel? What are you…? Where's…?"

"Not here, Father…" Gabe moved closer. "She's not here."

"Ha, Gabriel – you have returned, like me!" Rafael pointed at himself. "And this time you are angel-named, as am I!" He sounded triumphant, as if by being there Gabe had given him some kind of advantage.

The whole atmosphere inside the chapel changed. The power had shifted, and it hit Gabe like a gut punch that his arrival had been the catalyst, that he had allowed a switch to be thrown. He saw it now, with an awful clarity. Somehow Father Simon had managed to trap Rafael within the chapel walls, and his own unscheduled, unwanted appearance had royally messed it all up.

"No one sent me!" Gabe shouted, moving towards Father Simon, who looked drained and exhausted, like he had the heaviest of weights on his back. *Dead weight*, said the voice in his head.

"I found him, Gabriel…" said Father Simon, gasping for breath. He reached out for Gabe's arm and held on to him. "I finally found him, after much searching … and I discovered, as I thought – as I feared – that he had been thrown out of the Church for the disgrace of his many, terrible heretic sins. The evil things he did, Gabriel, I can't begin to tell you!"

"You don't have to, Father," Gabe said. He'd seen plenty and didn't have to be told anything about what Rafael could do. "Can I help?"

Father Simon didn't appear to have heard anything Gabe had said, his eyes round, staring at Rafael. "This man sacrificed the living, bathed in the blood of children, sold his eternal soul for forbidden knowledge. This man sinned like no other and for that was consigned to Hell. They tried to remove you from this Earth, Rafael! They failed, but where they failed *I* shall succeed! I *shall* succeed, Rafael!"

The dark, shadowy figure spun round in a circle, and as he came to a halt he held one hand up high. "I *am* Rafael Delacruz!" he yelled. "And your church, *any*one's church, means nothing to me… I am here to do nothing less than serve the Bringer of Light on Earth!"

Fireballs exploded in the air around Rafael. In the blasts of light Gabe saw he was holding what at first looked like a dripping piece of meat, and then he knew it wasn't just a piece of meat, it was a heart. And the table behind Rafael was an altar, with the body of a large dog on it.

"I am back here to open the eyes of a slumbering world and continue His work!" Rafael let the heart drizzle blood on to his face, then flung it behind him.

"His, and all the other heathen idols you worship!" Father Simon coughed and pulled himself back up to his full height, pointing at the sneering, gloating man in front of him. "As Isaiah says: 'How art thou fallen from heaven, Oh day-star, son of the morning!' – Lucifer by any other name! Satan the Great Adversary!"

"Your kind, you have your resurrection myths, and I have *my* reality…" Rafael, smiling as another burst of light shot up towards the roof beams. He thumped his chest with his other hand as he spoke. "I am His servant! And. I. Am. *Risen!*"

Gabe stared at Rafael in disbelief, the truth hitting him that, right there in front of him, was some kind of Dark Angel. He couldn't believe he'd just thought that.

It was insane, completely unthinkable. Or would be, if he hadn't totally lost his grip on reality. And right now he could feel the rope connecting him to the world outside this ancient chapel running through his fingers as if it had been greased. The world where he was just a kid at school, whose biggest problem until a few days ago had been how to deal with a fixated, bonehead of a dope dealer, not Satan's

Resurrected Servant on Earth. He had *got* to get his act together. He had to remember that he did not believe in any of this!

Then the doors to the chapel slammed shut behind him.

Chapter Thirty-One

Overhead the owl flew up to the small window set into the back wall, near the roof. It landed and sat, head on one side, observing. Gabe glanced over his shoulder and saw the coyotes, inside now and on the prowl, eyes fixed on him, their prey.

There was something almost human about the way these animals acted. He hadn't noticed before, but they appeared to have no fear at all. Instead there was a feeling of recognition, like they were saying, 'We know who you are, we know all about you.' Animals didn't do that, tame or wild. It was the stuff of bad dreams. Like the ones he'd been having ever since he'd found the gold. But this – here, now – this was not anything he was going to wake up from.

Gabe tried and failed to swallow. He wiped away the sweat that ran down from his forehead and looked at Father Simon. It was all down to him that the man had come here to deal with Rafael, exorcise him or whatever it was good priests did to evil priests. The Father was grimacing, like he was in a great deal of pain, and that had to be his fault too.

Cecil LeBarron and his client had died because of him. Stella was… He didn't want to think where Stella might be, but she was there because of him.

He, Gabe Mason, had to answer for all of it.

If he had never found the gold, none of this would have occurred, no one would have had their throats ripped out, the world wouldn't be going crazy and he and the Father would not be about to die.

"You, boy!"

Gabe turned his attention back to Rafael, astonished at the number of different thoughts a brain could process in such a short space of time, wondering when the torture would begin.

"Where is it – where is what belongs to me? What was taken from me should be returned!" Rafael, his head at a strange angle like he had a really bad crick in his neck, stared at Gabe, anger stoking the mad fire in his eyes. "You are my chosen one. I recognized you, that is why I *spared* you, boy! You were sent, you came to find me again … and you wished and prayed so hard. I knew you would come. You were born for these majestic days. Through you I have been reborn – you who will be anointed again, you who will now walk in my shadow forever, drink the blood of life with me and feel the last beat of a thousand *thousand* hearts! Why have you let me down?"

"I don't know you!" Gabe couldn't make any sense of what Rafael was saying – why was he making it sound like they'd met before? "I never wanted to be chosen, I never did!"

"Be *very* careful what you wish for, boy. A question cannot be *un*asked. A wish, once granted, can never be revoked." Rafael smiled. "And now I have you back, you are mine."

Rafael's mood seemed to change in the blink of an eye, one moment fired up with uncontained anger, the next placid and calm. It occurred to Gabe that maybe being brought back to life did that to a person.

"I told you!" Gabe screamed. "I *told* you I don't believe in you!"

"Did you not listen? Are you an *imbecile* – so stupid you cannot understand?" Rafael reared back. "I warned you, boy. I *showed* you what would happen if you do not do what I say... If I do not have what is mine returned to me. Yet still you came here empty-handed. Where *is* what is mine, boy? Where is it?"

Rafael was now shouting at Gabe; it felt like his words were physically hitting his face and chest, as if they were stones that Rafael was pelting him with. The pain in his head was beginning to grow, but it did more than just hurt. This time it made Gabe angry.

He had been angry at Janna's, but he'd also been frightened; fear had shut down all higher brain activity and allowed a primal instinct to take over. The anger Gabe could feel building in him now was different.

Call me 'boy' again, Rafael, and see what happens, Gabe thought.

Push me, Rafael, and I'll push back.

Threaten me, Rafael, and I will *fight back.*

This was a cool anger. Considered. Practical. And Gabe had no clue where it came from, but he knew it'd all be over if he didn't keep the man talking, keep him at a distance. Give himself space to think.

As plans went, that was all he had.

Chapter Thirty-Two

Fighting the urge to make a run for the doors, Gabe started moving himself in front of Father Simon. "Really, you don't know where your stuff is? I thought you said you were so powerful... Didn't you say that?"

All he had were his bare hands and whatever wits were left after everything he'd been through over the previous couple of days. He needed some way to level the playing field, give himself a fighting chance. Surely there *had* to be something here he could use? Had to be. Would Father Simon have come to the chapel to fight this evil jerk and *not* have brought with him the wherewithal to do the job? No, he wouldn't, that was just wrong.

"And if *you* don't know –" Gabe hoped he sounded a lot more confident than he felt – "then *I* can't help you..."

"You *will* help me, acolyte, you always have!"

Rafael brought his hands together, cupping the brilliant sphere of light that flared between them. He appeared amazed at his own power, staring at the blazing globe with a kind of hypnotized expression. The dazzle uplit his face, bleaching it bone-white, and cast a huge, dancing shadow on the wall behind him.

"You were my channel back to life, where I belong, and you are now here to serve unquestioningly. And, whatever you might like to think, that, boy, will *never* change." Rafael's eyes flared. "The Fates brought us together... The energy and passion of your youth reaching out and touching the wisdom and mastery of my ageless mind. It was our destiny to meet again, to carry on my work like we did before. Only this time there will be no mistakes!"

"Don't listen to his poisonous lies, Gabriel..." Father Simon hissed behind him. "Leave while you can, boy, this is my battle! I can defeat him, I can stop this from going any further, and it is far better that I do it on my own. Believe me, *far* better..."

The urge to do exactly as the Father told him, to bail right there and then, give way to his panic and run, was so, so tempting. But Gabe couldn't give up.

He had to try to find even the smallest chink in Rafael's armour.

Or die trying.

As he edged further in front of Father Simon he saw what was in the priest's left hand, which was hanging limply by his side. A large, ornate crucifix. And then on the floor he noticed a distinctive, square plastic bottle, its cap off next to it; the decorative blue label proudly declared it was FIJI WATER.

Shouldn't a priest be drinking holy water? Gabe thought, finding it hard to believe he'd still had an operational sense of the absurd.

The split second after having that thought, he realized what must be in the bottle. The next moment, Gabe was flinging himself sideways, awkwardly pivoting on the ball of his foot. As he crouched and spun he grabbed the cross from Father Simon's hand, then picked up the bottle and landed back on two feet. Turning, he faced Rafael and held the cross up high in front of him.

"You don't believe, boy!"

"No!" Gabe swung the bottle, watching as all the water left in it arced out across the chapel, molten silver in the air, and hit Rafael in the face. "But *you* do!"

The effect was instantaneous. Now the screeching started, a desperate razor-blade wail. But it wasn't in Gabe's head. It was echoing off the chapel walls and Gabe could hardly believe it when he saw Rafael clawing manically at his face.

The shock of seeing what he'd done stalled him for a moment, then he shook himself out of it, knowing that this might be his only chance to get out, get Father Simon away. Survive.

"Come on!" Gabe started backing towards the doors. "We gotta go, like *now*..."

"You go, Gabe, I can't, I haven't finished here." Father Simon reached into his trouser pocket and brought out a small book. "I *must* do this, I must send him back where he belongs, stop this terrible thing before it goes any further."

Gabe could feel what little control he'd managed to grab fading away fast as Rafael's shrieking began to ebb. As he wondered what it was the Father was trying to stop Rafael from doing, he saw the owl spread its wings and launch itself off from its perch. And behind him he heard a low growling from the coyotes. The enemy was on the move, time was running out and any minute now the game would be lost.

"Look, Father…"

But Father Simon had turned away and was holding a small book in his hand. He'd started to read out loud, his voice shaky but strong, his eyes wide. At first Gabe thought the priest had lost the plot and was babbling, then realized he must be speaking in Latin…

Chapter Thirty-Three

With every strange and incomprehensible word Father Simon spoke, Rafael jerked and quivered like he was a marionette being controlled by the world's twitchiest puppeteer. He was spitting too – dark green stuff – and his feet were rising off the ground. Horribly fascinated, Gabe couldn't take his eyes off the unfolding scene in front of him.

A rasping, chainsaw snarl jerked him back to reality, and he saw a coyote, jaws wide and slavering, sink his teeth into Father Simon just above the knee, taking him down like an old, lame stag. A moment later the other coyote was at his throat, the prayer book flying out of the Father's hand.

Stunned, Gabe nearly missed the owl diving straight at him from the rafters. Ducking for cover as the bird flew over, centimetres from his head, he dived towards Father Simon. Taking a wild kick, he felt his sneaker connect with one of the coyotes as the owl came back, claws out, for another go at him. This time he wasn't quick enough. His cheek and forehead got slashed, blood running into his eye and down his chin as the coyote he'd booted turned on him.

The owl wheeled in the air, readying to attack him again. Gabe knew he couldn't fend off both creatures. This had to be it. His final scene.

He heard the rush of air through feathers as the owl came in for a third strike.

He saw one of the coyotes, teeth bared, staring balefully at him.

He heard Father Simon's screaming stop, mid agonized wail, as the priest rolled on to his back; gouts of blood sprayed from his throat.

The Father was dead. Had to be. Bile rose in Gabe's throat, the acid stinging as he swallowed. The Father was dead. And he would be next.

He was aware of Rafael, his face blistered and scarred where the holy water had hit him. Aware that the man was beginning to take back control of his body as whatever effect Father Simon had had on him wore off.

In the outer edge of his vision he could see the owl.

Sensing the fight had gone out of its quarry, it was zeroing in for the kill, wings outstretched, talons aimed straight for Gabe's eyes.

Sometimes a body will react so fast that no one is more surprised by an action than the person doing it. Gabe had all but forgotten he was still holding the Father's crucifix, and was completely taken aback when his arm whipped upwards and the air filled with a silent explosion of feathers.

In the two, maybe three moments of silence that followed the Ninja move he didn't know he had in him, all Gabe could think was, if this had been a movie, it wouldn't be long before the end credits rolled.

"No kidding..." Gabe whispered to himself, letting the bloody crucifix drop to the ground.

Facing him, one to his left the other to his right, were the coyotes. Both were quivering with anger, hackles raised, spring-loaded for action. And between them stood Rafael, feet firmly back on the ground, totally in charge. His lips were curled, but he wasn't smiling.

"You, boy, *will* die ... and it will be so *exquisitely* painful that your flesh will sing with the glorious agony of it … and it *will* take such a long, long time. Oh, believe me, yes it will…" Now Rafael smiled, lips twisting upwards. "This I promise. Treachery such as yours cannot go unpunished, and this *will* happen, of that you should have no doubt. But not today. Not today. I have much work to do and you are to be spared until this work is done. After that, after you die, I shall spit on your shattered corpse and leave you for carrion."

There was nothing Gabe could say to that. What kind of response could there be to hearing, in such graphic detail, how he was going to die? He wasn't even sure what carrion actually was, but considering everything else Rafael had said, he figured it wasn't anything good.

He felt numb, unable to think straight no matter how hard he tried. This was Los Angeles. Outside this old building there was a whole world, a *real* world, where he belonged. Burger joints, movie houses, pizza parlours, shopping malls, all that good stuff. And he had a family, he had friends, there was school. People would miss him – heck, even Benny would miss him – he would be looked for. There was no way this maniac and his weird animal sidekicks could get away with killing Father Simon, and then killing him. Outside there were police, FBI, the CIA, whoever, people who upheld the law. Got the bad guys...

"We must go, and swiftly!"

Gabe blinked, Rafael's interruption stopping his train of thought. Go? He looked around the chapel at the carcass of the owl he'd killed and the coyotes who wanted to kill him, at Father Simon's mutilated body, lying in an expanding pool of blood. Yeah, he wanted to go too, but the only place he wanted to go was home.

Rafael strode over and took hold of Gabe's arm, his fingers tight as steel bands, and dragged Gabe across the shifting carpet of blood-spattered white feathers on the floor.

He was not going home.

Chapter Thirty-Four

"Where are you taking me?"

Rafael ignored the question and continued to march along the wide pathway through the graveyard. Gabe stumbled to keep up with him, the sentinel coyotes pacing either side of them, radiating hatred. Their message might have been silent, but it came loud and clear: *You killed our friend, and we will not forget.*

There wasn't even a hint of chill in the air, but Gabe was shivering like it was ten below zero. He'd completely lost control of his life – of what was left of his life – and was now slave to the lunatic dragging him off to who knew where. He did not want to die – slowly, or quickly – but it didn't look like it was going to be his choice.

Ahead were the wide, decorative iron gates of the cemetery entranceway. Cars were passing by, cars with drivers and passengers. When they got out on to the street, surely someone would see them? He could call for help, make it clear to anyone looking their way that he was being held against his will.

Out on the sidewalk it took a moment for Gabe to realize how very quiet it was, even for a Sunday morning. Up ahead he saw an SUV come round the corner, and as it got nearer Gabe could see it was full of people. He tried to scream, but nothing happened. Nothing happened because his mouth refused to open, like his lips had been super-glued together. He waved frantically, but no one gave him a first glance, let alone a second, didn't notice a man dragging some hysterical young guy along with him. Accompanied by coyotes? How could you *not* see that? It was like they were invisible.

"This is not your world now," Rafael said, seeming to read Gabe's mind. "You will never be a part of it again, boy. You … you are mine until I have done with you."

Rafael's grip on Gabe's arm tightened and he could feel the sensation of pins and needles in his fingers as the bloodstream became even more constricted.

"I have been touched by angels, I have talked with gods, walked with immortals. Nothing here can touch me, or what is mine. *I* will not be bound by the flimsy, *pathetic* rules of this time and place. I will follow other, more powerful and unchanging, dictates and decrees."

Gabe hadn't a clue what Rafael was rambling on about, but he could see they were making straight for the road, and it was clear Rafael was just going to walk straight into the traffic. And he had no option but to go with him.

Off the sidewalk now. Into the traffic lanes. Cars, trucks, vans, you name it, they were coming from both directions, but the drivers simply kept on driving. No honking horns, no screeching brakes, no squeal of rubber on tarmac. No dull thud as flesh and bone met a ton or more of pressed steel, plastic, toughened glass and aluminium engine block. Nothing.

And as they continued walking Gabe found the world around him fading away, dissolving like a watercolour painting in the rain.

Blurring.

Disintegrating.

Fading, light to dark.

Gabe looked down and could see though his hands,

through his pale, waning body. Had he become a ghost, died without realizing it? No such luck, not if Rafael's threats were to be taken seriously, and he kind of thought they had to be.

He didn't know where he was going but he didn't care, instead finding himself wondering if this was what being on drugs was like. He felt totally spaced and out of his head. Gone, and never coming back home. But strangest of all, for the first time in a long time, he didn't hurt or feel scared, he wasn't tired or angry. He felt calm and so completely and extraordinarily like himself. He was just Gabriel Mason, the person no one else really knew or ever would know. It was cool, so cool he never wanted it to stop.

But then the unwritten rule that life taught you, right from your very earliest days, kicked in. The one which stated: all good things, all of them, must come to an end.

Gabe felt himself shudder and wobble, like he was made out of jelly; light streamed in and reality poured over him, sucking itself back into his veins and bringing with it all the bad things it had felt so good to lose. He breathed in, gasping for air and his chest heaving, a drowning man who had just fought his way to the surface.

Standing on the sidewalk, next to Rafael, who still had him in his killer grip, Gabe saw they were outside Father Simon's place. Which was impossible. It was miles away from the Mission San Sebastian. He had to be hallucinating, or else … he was at a complete loss as to what else might have happened.

"Inside!"

Gabe staggered forward as Rafael roughly shoved him towards the rectory's front door. He stopped and looked over his shoulder. "What?"

"Go in." Rafael pointed. "Go in and get me what he left there, minion."

"But—" An electric shock arced across Gabe's brain, a blizzard of tiny bright lights flashing in front of him.

"Do as you have been told!"

"I don't…" Gabe staggered slightly, dizzy and confused. "Who d'you mean, what do you want?"

"I want the things you stole, cretin! I want the things you gave to your feeble priest."

"I've got no idea where they are."

"Seek and ye shall find, boy." Rafael leant forward, eyes glowing. "*Seek!*"

Chapter Thirty-Five

Gabe stood in the middle of Father Simon's study for a moment, wondering why Rafael hadn't just come in and got the gold pieces for himself, instead of sending him. Maybe the Father had cast a spell, or maybe done something more priest-like to the house, if that wasn't completely ridiculous. No, the more he thought about it, that must be it. Something was keeping Rafael from entering the rectory.

He reached up and felt the owl scratches on his face. They stung when he touched them, and he wondered for a second if he would be scarred for life. Yeah, like that was worth worrying about. He looked around the room that had become familiar to him in such a short time. He glanced at the desk the Father would never sit at again, the books he'd never consult, the bourbon he wouldn't drink.

The bourbon.

"Purely medicinal, man," Gabe said out loud. "Calms the nerves."

If there was anyone who needed their nerves calming he figured it was him. And maybe a shot would help straighten his head so he could think of a way out of this major pile of crap he'd gotten himself dropped into.

Yup, that was such a well known benefit of drinking alcohol.

The last thing he needed was to mess with his already messed-up head. As he turned his back on the bottle of bourbon in the cabinet he saw one of the coyotes, standing guard in the hallway. The loathing and contempt in its eyes rattled him for a moment, then he got a grip, walked over and slammed the study door shut in the coyote's blood-stained muzzle.

"See how good you are at turning doorknobs, mutt!"

Gabe went over to the desk and pulled open the top right-hand drawer, where he and Stella were supposed to have left the medallion. In one of the compartments he spotted a bunch of keys and picked them up, then sat down in the Father's black leatherette office chair and leant back.

Somewhere in this room were the gold pieces, all except the medallion, which was in Stella's camera bag. For safekeeping. Gabe sighed inwardly at the thought of what Rafael would do when he found something was missing, if the man didn't somehow know already. But he would have to deal with that when it happened. Right now the job was to find where Father Simon had put the stuff, then hand it over to Rafael. It was the last thing Gabe wanted to do, and what the Father had died trying to stop, but what was the alternative? Rafael would turn his brain to mush or worse if he didn't. And then kill him if he did anyway. A real lose-lose situation.

A noise out in the garden made him look round, to find the other coyote at the French windows. If an animal could look condescending, this one had it down. It yawned and licked its chops. Gabe got up and roughly drew the curtains, then went back to the desk knowing there was no way this was going to end well.

Gabe set to work, looking for the only logical place to hide something valuable. Somewhere that was locked shut. None of the desk drawers fitted the bill, and had nothing in them of any interest. Same with the two-drawer filing cabinet, and the next three cupboards he tried. At first he thought the door to the fourth cupboard might be stuck, then realized it wasn't and started trying to find the right key for it. He got it at the third try, the key sliding in sweetly and turning with a soft click. He pulled the door open, expecting anything but what he saw.

A safe. A black metal safe, locked up tight.

It wasn't the old type, with dials you had to spin backwards and forward, but the more modern kind, similar to the one in a hotel he'd stayed at once, a couple of years ago when they'd last been on a family holiday. It had a keypad, and needed a four-digit access code. Which he did not know.

Gabe sat back on his heels and looked up at the ceiling for help. And saw the crucifix on the wall, the scroll above the figure of Jesus with the letters 'INRI' on it. Could it possibly be *that* easy? He'd seen an article online that said a stupidly large number of people were so dumb they chose 123456 as their online security code as it was simple to remember. He didn't for one moment think the Father had been an idiot, but anything was worth a try...

Chapter Thirty-Six

Gabe reached for his cell phone to check which letters went with which numbers and stopped, kicking himself for not thinking about it before – he should be calling the cops! He had tapped 9-1-1 on the keypad before registering there was no signal showing. His shoulders sank. How Rafael had done it he didn't know, but he was trapped with no exit strategy.

"Shit-shit-shit…" Gabe checked the keypad again, then went back and knelt in front of the safe. He punched in the numbers relating to each letter – four, six, seven, four – and heard the chunking sound of the electronic lock disengaging. Despite the dire circumstances he smiled at his success; sure, it was a simple code, but not completely obvious.

Pulling open the safe door he was relieved to find the gold was there, on top of some papers and still loosely wrapped in his old duster. But next to it was something that took him by surprise. A handgun, in a black leather holster. Not entirely what he expected he'd find in a priest's safe, but then Father Simon was anything but your regular type of priest, having been some kind of a cop. Maybe the gun was a souvenir, or maybe it was down to the fact that, like the saying went, old habits died hard.

Gabe reached in and picked up the gold. The tingle that he felt run up his arm was unnerving, like a mild electric shock, and the sour, metallic taste in his mouth made him feel vaguely sick. He quickly put the gold pieces on the carpet next to him, then picked up the holster. Standing, he took the pistol out and looked at the L-shaped hunk of matte black metal sitting in the palm of his hand. The words 'SIG SAUER' were stamped into its short, thick barrel, the code 'P228' etched on the grip. At a guess it weighed about half a kilo, and it gave off the oily smell of a machine, a smell that reminded him of his dad's workbench. The gun looked used but well cared for.

He might not know very much about firearms, but there was an empty space in the pistol's grip where the magazine should go, and when he pulled back the top half of the barrel to cock the gun, there was nothing in the chamber. It wasn't loaded. Gabe pulled the trigger, but it wouldn't move. OK, OK … safety catch … the Father had left it on, even though the gun was empty.

Gabe looked the gun over and saw a lever at the top of the grip, right above where the thumb would be when it was held. It was angled upwards, so he pushed it down and pulled the trigger again. There was a solid, sharp clunk as metal struck metal and the firing pin hit an empty space. He looked back into the safe and, next to a squat cardboard box that said it contained 50 Aguila .40 S&W Full Metal Jacket cartridges, he spotted the magazine. Picking it up he could see the thing was full and slid it into the grip until it slotted fully in place. The extra weight gave the pistol even more authority.

Gabe pulled the top half of the barrel as far back as it would travel again and let it go. The hammer was now cocked, the safety off, the gun loaded and ready to fire. He could feel his heart thudding.

There were only two options open to him now. One, he could go back outside and give Rafael what he wanted, meekly handing over the gold. Or two, he could fight back and do the other thing.

This 'other thing' was an idea which had just occurred to him. And if he hesitated, Gabe knew it would never happen. Not in a million years. He'd just roll over and Rafael would win. It was his choice.

What was it they said? 'Damned if you do, and damned if you don't?' That was him. That was where he was.

He looked at the seemingly insignificant bundle on the carpet, wishing he'd never seen what was in it, or had somehow known to leave well enough alone. Oh the joy of 20/20 hindsight.

He bent down and picked up the gold.

Chapter Thirty-Seven

Gabe stood in front of the study door. This was, in a way, like he vividly remembered feeling when he'd been about to dive from the top board at the pool off Huston Street for the first time in his life. Nervous hadn't been the half of it, more like utterly petrified. Standing on the board, toes curled over the edge, he'd felt it was possibly the last thing he would do in his life, because it was so obvious nothing was going to stop him from slicing through the water like a dropped knife, after which his head would undoubtedly crack open on the bottom of the pool. DOA, right? But his friends had been watching, they'd all done it and survived, so he couldn't back down. And he had lived to tell the tale.

There was only one way to find out if that would be true this time.

He reached out and took hold of the doorknob. His palm was so sweaty it was hard to grip and he wiped his hand on his jeans. Then one twist and the door was open.

A millisecond after Gabe pulled the trigger the SIG bucked in his hand like it was as shocked as he was at what it had just done. The explosion was deafening and the place filled with a smell kind of like Fourth of July fireworks, but way more intense. The coyote lay in a crumpled heap on the floor, its brains and bits of fur and skull were spattered all over the wall, the pink tip of its tongue poking out of its mouth. Gabe stepped over the limp carcass and walked on down the hall.

He'd never fired a gun before.

He'd never shot anything before.

He felt … nothing.

He wondered how he'd be feeling now if it had been a person not an animal that he'd shot and killed.

Up ahead the front door was half open, but that was where Rafael would be expecting him to appear. Instead, Gabe dodged to his left, into a room kitted out like a reception, which, if he remembered correctly, had a bay window.

It did, and through the side pane he saw Rafael, a perplexed expression twisting his scarred face. Gabe didn't think, just pointed the gun and fired, the glass shattering into a hail of shards and splinters that blew outwards. He managed to squeeze off three more shots as he tried to follow Rafael's dive for cover behind a low hedge, but had no way of knowing if any of the bullets had hit their intended target. He didn't care. This, what he was doing now, this *had* to attract attention… Multiple gunshots being fired, shattering the peace and quiet at nice, kind Father Simon's rectory? On a Sunday morning? This being LA, he figured it was unlikely anyone was going to risk actually coming out to see what the problem was, but if it didn't spook the entire neighbourhood and start to get the Emergency Services calls made, well, he didn't know what would.

There had been no time to come up with a carefully engineered master plan, Gabe just figuring he'd go with the principal that the best form of defence was attack. So far it had worked for him – one coyote down, one to go, and he'd made Rafael jump. Pretty good, pretty good. But before the element of surprise wore off, and he lost whatever small advantage it had given him, he had to get out of the building, and the gaping hole in the window beckoned.

Jagged glass teeth stuck out, waiting to bite him, but there was probably enough space to make an exit, if he was careful. Using the gun barrel to knock a couple of stiletto spikes from the bottom of the window frame, Gabe eased his way through the gap as quickly as he dared, making it unscathed. He was halfway down the path to the sidewalk when Rafael reappeared.

He came out from behind the hedge, swaying slightly. A dark red stain ran down one side of his face, then Gabe noticed he was gripping his right arm, just below the shoulder. So the man's claim that he'd been touched by angels, which meant nothing could harm him, was a load of bull. And also, Gabe wasn't such a bad shot.

Gabe had brought the gun up again and was taking a two-handed aim at Rafael's face when a metallic pain scythed through his head. He dropped the gun and collapsed to the ground. Lying rigid on the path, his eyes wide open, Gabe saw Rafael coming towards him. The agony ramped up with every step the man got closer, in the end so bad that Gabe was beyond screaming.

The slow death had begun.

"Where is it, boy?" Rafael held out his right hand; it was shaking slightly and blood had dribbled on to his palm. "*Where* is it?"

Like a tap had been turned off, the pain disappeared and Gabe sucked in air. "Still there… Still in the house…"

"What? *What?!*" The pain returned and Rafael reached down with his bloody hand, grabbed the neck of Gabe's T-shirt and hauled him up off the ground like he weighed next to nothing. Upright, feet only just touching the path, Gabe was only centimetres away from Rafael's face and was finding it hard to breathe. "Go back and get it!" Spittle flecked Rafael's thin lips. "Do as you have been told!"

"No…" Gabe was beyond caring what happened to him and looked away from Rafael. The man's face was not the last thing he wanted to see before he died.

Staring over Rafael's shoulder, across into the small park opposite, Gabe thought he must be delirious. Right there, on the other side of the street, a pale grey Chevy van was pulling up.

Chapter Thirty-Eight

Gabe watched as Benny, a lit cigarette stuck in his mouth, turned round and looked out of the van's side window at nothing in particular. Saw Benny catch sight of him, his jaw dropping in total cartoon style, the cigarette falling out. All the time Rafael, wild-eyed, was still yelling and shaking him like he was some raggedy fairground kewpie doll.

As Benny scrabbled to find the cigarette that was now down between his legs, the van's sliding rear door opened and Gabe watched Stella, holding her camera bag, being pushed out by Nate. Disoriented, she looked around to find out where she was. Her eyes locked on to Gabe's and she screamed his name.

Rafael stopped yelling and cocked his head to one side, listening intently, like a bird. Letting Gabe go, he turned on his heels and walked towards the van.

"Something is there, this I know – and *you* have it!" Rafael pointed a blood-stained finger directly at Benny. "You have something that is mine, give it to me *now*!"

As fried as Gabe's brain cells were, a few still functioned well enough to work out that Benny had found the medallion. And Rafael had zoned in on the fact that there was a piece of his gold somewhere in the van. Which, unlike the rectory, was not protected by any prayers that Father Simon might have said.

"Man, I don't got nothing in the world you need." Benny, cigarette back in place, blew smoke out of the window. "What you *look* like you need is a trip to the ER, guy, blood dripping off of you every damn where. My man Gabe do that to you? He must be a whole lot more of a dangerous-type person than I thought." Benny looked away. "Right, Scotty?"

"Give it to me *now*!"

"Screw you, mister…"

As Gabe bent down to pick up the gun he caught sight of a silver car … a Toyota. Stella's Toyota? He shook his head. No it couldn't be as he'd driven her car to the Mission, where it still had to be. Then the Toyota was forgotten, his attention grabbed by a wailing sound in the distance… OK, this was good.

261

Sirens. At last, the real cavalry. He stood back up, holding the gun loosely, and felt someone's hand on his shoulder. Stella was right there, staring at him. She looked pale and very scared.

"Gabe… What happened to you? Is Father Simon here?"

Gabe shook his head. Relief that Stella seemed to be fine hit him like a shot of adrenaline, clearing his head.

"Where is he?"

"It's, you know, kinda complicated…" There was no way he could even begin to tell her about the incident at the old San Sebastian chapel, not right now. "Are you OK, did Benny hurt you?"

"No… No, he didn't—" Stella broke off mid-sentence, registering what Gabe was holding. "Where did you get that?"

"That's kinda complicated too."

The sirens were getting nearer. Across the street the coyote had appeared next to Rafael, and from the shouting and the ruckus, the confrontation with Benny looked like it had ratcheted up and was about to go nuclear any second.

There are moments when panic takes over and

rational actions don't have a rat's chance. And there are times, in the middle of total chaos, when there's a moment of clear, lucid thinking.

In that moment Gabe figured the next move. They had to leave before the cops arrived, and before Rafael turned his attention back on to him. Because if the cops found him at the scene of a break-in, a burglary *and* a shooting there was no way he wasn't going to be in the deepest of deep shit.

And if Rafael got him, he'd be a dead guy.

Simple choice.

"We have to go, Stella, right now!" Gabe slipped the safety catch on and shoved the gun down the back of his jeans. Like it was something he'd been doing all his life. "Is there another way out of here, like through the garden?"

"Yes, but—"

"I'll explain everything, I promise, but we *have* to go. It'll get real bad any minute and the cops can't find me here…"

Before Gabe could say any more the coyote leapt into the van. At the same time, Rafael reached through the open passenger-side window. The air was filled with tortured screams, snarls and bright flashes of light. Then it was all over, the violence quick and very bloody.

Gabe saw Rafael step back from the van, his hands red, his smile like a cut. Benny had slumped forward, his door freshly decorated with a dribbling crimson splatter. He also caught a glimpse of Scotty and Nate abandoning ship like the rats they were.

For the longest moment nothing happened.

Stella clung to Gabe.

The coyote reappeared, glaring daggers.

Rafael leered.

And the pain came back. Gabe doubled over, clutching his head.

Screeching brakes announced the arrival of the cops. A squad car pulled up, two officers jumping out of the black and white. Definitely time to be elsewhere.

"Gabe? We *have* to go!" Stella grabbed his arm and started to run, pulling him after her.

Chapter Thirty-Nine

Gabe and Stella hadn't even made it to the back of the Father's house.

When the cops had finally turned up it wasn't in a solitary black and white, more like a squadron of squad cars. They'd been stopped by a heavily armed member of the SWAT team that had also arrived and it wasn't long before someone noticed the gun.

Gabe had been at the police station for twenty minutes, possibly half an hour now, most of the time spent sitting on his own in a holding cell. He couldn't see a clock anywhere and they'd taken his phone off him. He was surprised he still had his shoelaces and belt. The uniform cop had told him he'd be dealt with 'as and when'. Scare tactics, he assumed. And they were working, like being put in handcuffs had.

He was managing to hold it together. Just about. He wished he knew what had happened to Stella as they'd been put in separate cruisers back at the rectory. But he figured, as she wasn't the one who had been found with a recently fired handgun stuck down the back of her jeans, she'd be in a whole heap less trouble than he most assuredly was.

There were definite advantages to being behind bars, though. Like the fact that he was safe and there was no way Rafael could get to him. He wasn't going to die. Not today, anyway. Gabe wondered where the man was now. Hopefully strapped into a straitjacket, locked up in a padded cell. He was responsible for at least four murders, maybe more if Scotty and Nate hadn't made it. He was an evil, *evil* sunnuvabitch and should never see the light of day again. Hopefully, he'd be headed directly for Death Row and a one-way ticket back to where he'd come from.

Back where he'd come from... The words made Gabe think about Father Simon. About how the priest had told Gabe that he was probably responsible for Rafael being here. He did not want to believe that was true, but wondered if he'd ever be able to convince himself it wasn't. What did he actually believe in? All he had believed, before, was that he had to try and help his family out of trouble, and it had got him into more strife than he could ever have imagined. He wondered if Stella, because she went to church, would look at this any different.

Whatever there was in store down the road – whatever charges the police threw at him, whatever his parents decided was an apt punishment – it would be a walk in the park compared to the heinous things Rafael had threatened to do to him.

Through the bars, in the larger cell next to his, he could see a trio of Saturday night drunks sprawled on the benches, sleeping off their respective big nights out. Two of them looked and smelled like they were regulars. The third not so much, as he must have started the night being dressed quite smartly. His evening had obviously not ended in the way he had originally intended it to. All three were mumbling and dribbling. With intermittent raucous snoring and the occasional loud fart thrown in for good measure. It was like he was in a 'Please drink responsibly' alcohol awareness advertisement.

Gabe, sitting as far away as he could get from his neighbours, stared through the bars of the cell at a large room with a grid of untidy desks and cubicles.

It was empty at the moment, though that was probably because it was a Sunday. Saturday night it must've been a zoo, and where he and Stella could have ended up if they'd been caught breaking into Morrison.

Father Simon came to the front of Gabe's mind again. None of the people Rafael had killed had deserved to die, except possibly Benny, but the Father least of all. Gabe thought about him, lying on the floor of that old chapel, another dead body in the Mission graveyard. What a waste. He had been a good man and had not deserved to end his life like that. Gabe wished he'd been a better shot and managed to do more than just wing Rafael.

He knew he was going to be asked so many questions, and that the truthful answers to some of them were going to make *him* sound like the crazy person. Right now, he couldn't care less if it did. Maybe it was him who was the mad one. But at least he'd stepped up and managed to stop Rafael from getting his hands on the gold artefacts, whatever he wanted them for. They were back in Father Simon's safe and there was no way Rafael was going in there. He began to rerun what had happened at the rectory, trying to imagine what it might look like to the cops.

Gabe wondered how he was going to explain what he'd been doing there – how he'd got the gun, why he'd shot Rafael and a coyote. He thought about what Stella might've already told the cops. Would their stories match up? Somehow he doubted it.

Gabe heard a door open and looked over to see a uniform ushering in a guy, late twenties maybe, spiky, pale ginger hair and a close-trimmed beard, sunglasses pushed up on to his head. The door swung shut behind them, the uniform directing the guy over to one of the tidier desks about eight, maybe ten metres away. The newcomer had a surly look about him and it seemed to Gabe that this wasn't the first time he'd been in this situation.

"Siddown." The cop nodded at a metal chair by the side of the desk.

"What?"

Gabe saw the guy's annoyed expression as the uniform cuffed one wrist to the desk.

"I said, you sit your ass down there. Detective Baring told me to tell you, don't touch nothing,

269

don't do nothing, don't speak to nobody don't speak to you first. Clear?"

Not waiting for an answer, the uniform walked off and Gabe saw the guy nod and slowly sit down on the chair, facing away from him. After angrily yanking at the cuffs he finally turned round to check behind him. Taking in the cell with the sleeping, snoring drunks first, he finally looked at Gabe.

"What the hell *you* do to get locked up?" The man sat back, lightly drumming his fingers on the desk.

"You wouldn't believe me if I told you."

"Try me."

"Really, I don't have the energy right now…"

The man was about to reply when the door he'd been brought through was pushed open again. Gabe watched a plain-clothes detective stride into the room and make a beeline for the cells. He recognized him as somebody he'd seen, fleetingly, outside the rectory, but there was something else about him that definitely made him kind of eerily familiar. The man was staring at him in a very off way as he came across the room.

Those eyes…

Gabe couldn't believe what he was thinking. It wasn't possible. Except that should have been true of so much of what had already happened.

Those eyes…

There was a fire in them that he'd seen before. Gabe pushed himself as far back in the cell as he could.

Somehow it was Rafael Delacruz.

Gabe shot a glance at the man sitting over by the desk, but what could he do? Then Rafael was opening the cell door and coming in. Gabe wanted to shout, but the sound stayed trapped in his throat. Without a word, Rafael walked over and grabbed Gabe's arm, pulled him upright and started to drag him out of the cell. One of the guys in the tank stirred, but then turned over and began to snore even louder than before. It was like some kind of surreal mime performance, in an almost-empty theatre.

Helpless, there was nothing Gabe could do but go where Rafael was taking him. He tried to look over at the guy cuffed to the desk but his head wouldn't cooperate. And the next thing he knew he was out in the corridor.

Chapter Forty

The door to the squad room banged open and a plain-clothes officer, along with a couple of uniforms came into the room. Their jokey, light-hearted banter stopped dead and in the silence the trio stared at the empty holding cell, its sliding gate as wide open as their mouths.

"Haskins?" The plain-clothes turned angrily on one of the uniforms, his arms spread out. "*Huh?*"

"I locked that, sir! Honest to…"

"He did, Mr de Soto." The other uniform pointed to his colleague. "I was there. I saw him, sir."

"Then how the hell…?" The detective, de Soto, caught sight of a bored-looking man, sunglasses pushed up on his head, sitting cuffed to a desk. "Who're you, what're you doing here on your own? You know anything about this clusterdump of a disappearing act?"

"Me?" The man shook his head. "No, I got

brought back to the station and told to wait here for Detective Baring."

"How long you been here?" Det. de Soto hurried through the warren of desks, pointing over at the holding cell. "Was he there – the kid – when you got brought in?"

"Sure." The man nodded, looking up at de Soto, standing right next to him and glaring.

"Well, where'd he go? How'd he get out?"

"He went out the way you just came in." The man's neck hurt looking up at the cop. "One of you guys arrived, unlocked the cell, took him away."

"One of us? A cop?" de Soto frowned, his lower lip jutting out like a shelf. "A uniform?"

"No, he was a suit, like you," the man shrugged, all noncommittal, but his eyes flicked towards the door. "Had to be a cop, right?"

Gabe knew it was all over. His world had flipped back into madness and with every step he took his hopes for a future evaporated.

Rafael had somehow managed to switch bodies, find a new person to inhabit. A cop, a detective.

273

Just an ordinary guy in a slightly wrinkled grey suit. Perfect. So he'd simply been able to walk into the station house and spirit him away.

Once Rafael had stepped out of the station house, it had been kind of a repeat performance of what had happened at the cemetery, when they'd walked straight into the traffic. There was another blurred, hitting-light-speed moment when he went all Zen and blissful, only to end up somewhere else entirely. And just like the first time, when he looked round to see where he was, Gabe found himself, once again, back outside the rectory.

The street looked like a mini war zone. Yellow and black tape had been strung across it either side of the rectory, effectively blocking off all access, and Benny's mobile office, the blood-spattered Chevy, was still there. As far as he could see, though, no sign of Benny. Crime-scene techs were everywhere, plus various plain-clothes and uniformed officers, all the activity being watched over by a crowd of neighbourhood rubberneckers. The very same people, it occurred to Gabe, who had been so conspicuous by their absence when they might have been of some help.

"And now −" Rafael's fingers dug into Gabe's arm − "this time you *will* do what I told you to do before... You are to go and get what belongs to me."

Gabe felt his resistance drain away as Rafael started walking towards the rectory with him. He lifted up the tape barrier with his free hand and they were in the cordoned off no-go area. On the radar. A uniform noticed them and came across, the expression on his face part recognition, part puzzlement.

"Detective Nicholls?" The officer stopped a few metres away, glancing from Rafael to Gabe, not sure what was going on. "Can I, uh... Can I help?"

"Yes, you can." Rafael pushed Gabe forward. "As you know, he left something in the house, yes?"

Gabe could feel the power radiating off Rafael. He watched the cop, his name badge saying he was called Beaumont, and saw his face blanking. Right then he knew Rafael had got him completely under his control.

"Yes, sir." Officer Beaumont's voice sounded flat, robotic. "Of course he did."

"Good. I have other business to attend to, so please see he goes in and retrieves it."

"Yes, sir, right away, sir." Officer Beaumont came over and took Gabe's arm, firmly.

"And make sure no one stops him." Rafael finally let go of Gabe. "No one."

"Yes, sir…"

Det. de Soto watched the red-headed perp being led away, taken out of the squad room. He'd apparently been picked up because he was accused of running some kind of credit-card scam, and he definitely wouldn't come high on anyone's list as a reliable witness. But he was the only person who had seen what had gone down, seen the boy being … de Soto shook his head, not even wanting to think the word 'kidnapped'. Removed from police custody was a better spin.

Except that the perp had pos-i-*tively* identified the person doing the removing as Det. Steve Nicholls, confirming beyond any reasonable doubt the video-surveillance evidence, plus the fact that the detective's car was missing from the pool. All of which was just plain ridiculous. He'd known Nicholls for at least eight or nine years, and while the man was no Sherlock Holmes, he was a reasonable enough detective and a decent, stand-up guy. Unless he'd had a total meltdown, this was not the kind of thing he would do.

But there was no getting round the fact that the kid, a material witness who had been found with a recently fired gun at the scene of a crime, was gone, and Nicholls was the one who had taken him.

Det. de Soto took a deep breath, closed his eyes for a second, then snapped his fingers. "OK, listen up … check we have the correct registration and put out a BOLO… Say it's a 10-57 and no action to be taken, just report where they are. Go-go-go!"

The squad room exploded into action. One of their own was out there, with the missing boy, and everyone had a job to do.

Chapter Forty-One

It wasn't every day, Anton thought, that your friend got himself arrested. But that's what the word was on Gabe, and that girl he'd seen him with, Stella. Plus Benny Gueterro was reckoned to be dead! Not that Anton believed everything he saw on the Net. Anyone could post any old garbage, and frequently did, but he couldn't just sit around and wait to find out what had really gone down. The moment he'd heard the news he'd fired up his scooter and buzzed over to the place it was all supposed to have happened, next to the big Catholic church.

When he got there, crime-scene tape blocked off the street either side of one particular house, which he could see had a busted-out front window. There was a lot of to-and-fro stuff going on, techs in their paper suits on pick-up-and-bag duty, techs taking pictures, flashes going off, and other cops making busy.

The main attraction was a pale grey Chevy that Anton recognized, which was parked kind of opposite the cordoned-off house. The front passenger door was liberally spattered with what was either red paint or, more likely given the circumstances, blood. So all the tattle about Benny having got his looked like it was true; he really hoped the same wasn't the case with Gabe being arrested.

Anton found a place to leave his scooter, locked the helmet under the seat and pushed his way to the front of the gawkers. A few minutes later he noticed a beige-coloured saloon pull up the other side of the tape from where he was standing, but he didn't pay it much attention until he saw who got out on the passenger side.

Gabe.

He was with some guy in a suit, he supposed it must be a detective, and he looked totally spaced, like he was stoned and not focusing on anything. Except Gabe didn't do that stuff.

Anton waved, but Gabe didn't respond. He thought about shouting out his friend's name, but something stopped him. Standing close to the yellow and black tape barrier he watched his friend walk off with a uniformed officer and disappear inside the house with the busted window.

Gabe and a blank-faced Officer Beaumont walked across the street; no one they passed even looked their way. They went down the path to the rectory's open front door, and into the house, which still held a faint aroma he recognized as gun smoke. Gabe could see down the corridor into Father Simon's room. There were people in there, and he was just supposed to stroll in and take away what they would no doubt consider evidence? How was *that* ever going to work?

Officer Beaumont carried on walking, stopping once they were in the study, where the two techs and a plain-clothes all looked up from what they were doing at the same time.

"OK, officer –" the plain-clothes, sitting at the Father's desk, pointed at Gabe – "what's this all about? Shouldn't he be back at the station?"

"He left something… He has to retrieve it."

"Retrieve?" The plain-clothes got up, cracking a half smile. "Is he a dog?"

Officer Beaumont let go of Gabe, pushing him slightly. "No one should stop him."

Wondering if this was what sleepwalking was like – seeing everything, but not being able to control anything you were doing – Gabe found himself going over to the open cupboard where the safe was and kneeling down in front of it. He looked up quickly at the picture on the wall, punched in the four-digit code and pulled open the door. Behind him he heard the sounds of a scuffle breaking out.

"What the hell's he doing?" The plain-clothes was turning angry now.

"Do not stop him," Officer Beaumont said, sounding like he was reading badly from a script. "He left something in the house, which he must retrieve."

Gabe reached in and picked up the gold... Felt the energy surge in the palm of his hand and pulse up his arm, like this evil treasure trove was aware he had come back to get it. He didn't want to stand up but he didn't have a choice, Rafael wasn't taking any chances this time and there was no way Gabe wasn't going to do what he'd been told. As he turned he saw the two techs, scared rigid, their eyes darting between him and the showdown between plain-clothes and Officer Beaumont.

"Stand back, officer – stand back and stand down. That's an order!"

Looking over his shoulder, Gabe saw the plain-clothes reaching into his jacket. Saw Officer Beaumont get to his handgun first and not even hesitate for a second before firing once … twice.

An invisible punch flung the plain-clothes backwards like he was a doll, a gout of blood erupting as the bullets exited out of his back, Officer Beaumont straight away turning the smoking barrel of his gun round at the techs.

"You take him, officer." One of the techs, eyes wide, was nodding at Gabe. "Really, take the kid, we got no problem with—"

Gabe could only watch, horrified at what was playing out. He saw Officer Beaumont shoot the first tech, then the second, both in the chest. Trapped in his own body, Gabe couldn't even close his eyes. Forcing himself to stare at the carpet, he tried to ignore the blood spatter on it. The phrase 'in cold blood' sprang to mind as the perfect description of the officer's kill spree. It was clinical, heartless, but Gabe had no doubt that was because, like him, the officer couldn't help what he was doing.

"You must go." Officer Beaumont jabbed a finger at the door. "Go back now, he is waiting. No one will stop you."

Gabe started walking, trying to ignore the three corpses sprawled around the room. What he should be doing was making a run for it, out through the open French windows and across the small slate-paved terrace. If only he could break the vice-like mental grip Rafael had on him, maybe this time he'd have a chance to get away. Except that was not going to happen. The only direction he was going was back up the corridor and out on to the street.

Anton watched the guy who had arrived with Gabe get back in his beige saloon. He assumed he was going to find somewhere to park it, but instead he reversed into a driveway and turned the car so it was facing back down the street. Like he was waiting for Gabe to return. Anton turned and, keys in hand, ran back to where he'd left his scooter…

Chapter Forty-Two

The last thing Gabe remembered clearly was walking back out of the rectory with the gold. He wasn't sure of the time, but thought it had probably been early afternoon. Now it was getting late and the darkness was pressing down on him, making the air heavy and difficult to breathe.

He was standing next to a car, Rafael a few feet away. The car, a nondescript red Nissan hatchback, was parked on a street that seemed familiar, and it finally dawned on Gabe that this was because it was the street the Mission San Sebastian was on. He glanced at the Nissan, aware he could hear the *tick-tick-tick* noise an engine makes when it's cooling down, and had a major 'two plus two equals…' moment.

How stupid could he have been? It was blindingly obvious that he hadn't been having *any* weird out-of-body, psychic experiences after all… That Rafael had been hypnotizing him, putting him into some sort of trance, which explained the silver Toyota he'd seen outside Father Simon's. It *was* Stella's, it was how Rafael had got him there from the Mission, and all the feelings he'd had that he'd been soul-flying in the psychic planes were all a total figment of his jazzed imagination.

So here he was, back at the Mission. And there was only one place here Rafael would want to go with the gold. The chapel.

Gabe focused on Rafael, who had moved to the back of the car and was opening the boot. He was a prisoner, but one with no visible chains holding him, and his captor could make him do anything he wanted. Bile rose in his throat, the pure, acid hatred of this man and what he was doing to him made real. He tried to get rid of the bitter taste, but it wouldn't go away.

Rafael slammed the hatchback closed and Gabe saw he was holding a shovel. Right there and then he knew, just totally knew, he would be made to use it to dig his own grave. A sense of absolute desolation washed over him.

"You had your chance to join me once more, but instead you turned against me!" Rafael said, interrupting Gabe's thoughts. "You had a chance, a chance few are *ever* offered, to be a part of a new beginning – because *this* time I shall succeed! Blood will flow, souls will be collected, faith will be redefined and those who choose not to follow will be destined for the eternal void!"

There was so much electricity in the air it felt as if every hair on Gabe's body was standing bolt upright. The man's power seemed to be growing by the minute, making Gabe wonder where it could possibly end. Father Simon had told him that he had somehow brought Rafael's spirit back from the past, a past he had dreamed about in such detail it had seemed like he really was there himself. And now here was Rafael insisting that he *had* been there, a witness to his terrible beginnings and now a participant in whatever he had planned for the future. But why him?

"Destiny. That is why, boy."

Gabe flinched, shocked by the realization that Rafael could not only make him do what he wanted, he knew everything that he was thinking. There really was no escape.

"Death is just a part of the process of living, and it

does not have to be an end to life. I have work to do on this stage which I was not allowed to finish, but I long ago discovered there are ways back. You and I have history, boy, no matter how much you might deny it, and you are here to help me finish. Whether you like it or not."

"I told you, I don't believe any of this…" Gabe wished he sounded more convincing.

"And I don't care what you believe, boy."

Gabe felt a shiver run down his spine. "What are you going to do?"

"Life is a circle." Rafael came round the car and took hold of Gabe's shoulder, pushing him to move towards the chapel. "It starts and ends at the same place, with the beat of a heart. Fools believe there is only One True Way, one power who can control the chaos of this never-ending spiral – but they are wrong! *I* am back to finish what I started."

"What did you start?"

"The cleansing. The end of everything here and now, which is necessary to allow the start of everything else – the start of the Next Time. And the last thing you will do before you die is understand all this, understand that the opposite of Good is not

287

Evil, and the opposite of Light is not Dark. That is a lie. These notions are simply two sides of the same thing, like a coin." Rafael reached into his pocket and held up a quarter, which glinted in the street light. "Life, as it is with this coin, is neither good nor bad, it is neutral. It all depends on your point of view…" Rafael flicked the coin with his thumb and Gabe watched it fly upwards, spinning so fast it was a blur. Rafael plucked it out of the air before it hit the ground. "Like this coin, life is all about what you do with it, how you choose to spend it."

Some way down the street, Anton experienced a strong sense of déjà vu as he watched Gabe and whoever the guy with him was. This was the same as when he'd kind of spied on Gabe when he'd gone to meet Benny. He'd felt bad then, but now it was different. Now his friend really was in trouble. Anton had figured it out earlier on, the moment he'd seen Gabe standing with the plain-clothes guy and then going into the rectory with the other police officer. That gut hunch was why he'd made the split-second decision to try to follow them and see where they went. He'd got a tankful of gas, nothing else to do and a friend in need. Enough said.

It hadn't been easy, but he'd stuck with it and been careful to hang back as far as he could, blending in with the Sunday traffic. And he knew for a fact, as a scooter rider, that what he had going for him was that he was as close to invisible to car drivers anyway.

Not long after the guy had driven Gabe away from the crime scene, he'd peeled off into the parking lot of a bunch of big stores where Anton had seen him dump the beige saloon right at the back and boost a truck. A couple of hours of seemingly aimless driving later he'd done almost exactly the same thing and swapped the truck for a red hatchback. And now he was taking Gabe across the road towards some kind of historic-looking church.

Anton hadn't called anyone up till now, as at first he'd thought the guy he was with was a cop, so there was no reason to. Now he wasn't so sure. Gabe hadn't looked to be in any danger before, but what was this guy doing taking him off to some church with a spade? He almost called 911, but stopped at the last moment. How long was it going to take for him to convince someone with enough authority to take his story seriously? *Way* too long was the answer to that question. Locking the scooter he slipped into the lengthening shadows and started to follow after Gabe.

Chapter Forty-Three

As he trudged along the wide path that led to the old chapel, Gabe realized something was missing. Fear. He wasn't scared. At least not in the kind of pant-wetting way he'd assumed you would be when you were staring the moment of your own death in the face. He didn't feel particularly heroic or fearless, either, but maybe you just weren't that frightened when something was inevitable. Turned out it simply made you realistic.

Rafael had been graphically clear that he was going to die, and Gabe was pretty sure, barring a miracle, that that's what was going to happen. Because he did not believe in miracles. He didn't want to die, he wanted to live, but it just wasn't going to go that way. Rafael had trapped him inside himself. He could see, hear, smell, but he couldn't *do*. He was nothing more than Rafael's puppet.

The sky was getting darker now; a razor-edged sliver of moon was hanging like a sharp warning in the deep blue border between night and day. A fevered excitement seemed to radiate off Rafael and Gabe could feel it, an almost physical force pushing him forward.

And then he was aware of shadows moving, off to the left and right. People? It looked like there were men and women coming through the cemetery, walking in the same direction they were... An overpowering sense of dread filled Gabe at the thought that Rafael might be responsible for making the long-dead residents of this place come back to life – was *that* his plan?

"They are not dead. I have gathered them to come and bear witness to the beginning of the Next Time," Rafael answered Gabe's unspoken question. "You found me, boy, but *I* found *them*. They answered my calls and they have come."

Gabe could feel a not so subtle change in the air, as if every living thing was nervously waiting for something extraordinary to happen, like the tense calm before a big storm broke, but much edgier. The indigo curtain that joined the sky to the horizon had grown; it was turning an oily black, and a sickly warm breeze feathered in carrying with it the strangest brew of smells, none of which Gabe could immediately identify. Then, up ahead, darker against the charcoal-night backdrop, he saw the silhouette of the chapel.

The shadowy people were much closer to them now – moonlit, pale figures, animated statues walking quietly through the grey memorial stones. They all had the same blank expression he'd seen on the face of the cop at Father Simon's place. Gabe had no idea how Rafael had managed to control all these people, how he'd got them to leave wherever they'd been and join him here, but the man's powers seemed to have grown by the moment since he'd come back. And now he had the gold. Now he had the gold, and Gabe didn't even want to think what he might be able to do.

Then, like a green shoot in a desert, an idea, a vain hope, occurred to him. How much of what he was seeing and feeling was actually real, and how much was it Rafael messing with him? The hope promptly died.

This was happening, and there was no way out for him.

No one was here to help.

As they approached the chapel, random images of the last time he'd been there barged their way into his head. Rafael with something that looked like a bloody heart in his fist... Father Simon's torn and savaged body... The delicate snowfall of feathers after he had killed the owl... The holy water arcing like lightning through the air and striking Rafael's face... The coyotes...

Gabe realized he hadn't seen the remaining coyote since Rafael had killed Benny. If he could have stopped and looked around for it he would have, but it wasn't up to him; all he could do was put one foot in front of the other, his remaining lifespan shortening with each step. It was hot for this late in the day, and Gabe was aware of his own rank sweat and the tension knots in his shoulders. Everything ached. He wasn't going to die young and leave a beautiful corpse; he was going to die and leave a tired, worn-out and stinking one.

He was thinking how stupid it was to waste precious time fretting about his personal hygiene when with no warning Rafael made him come to an abrupt halt; standing rock-rigid about twenty metres from the chapel doors, Gabe watched Rafael walk in front of him and motion silently to the group of followers. In the gloom Gabe couldn't see exactly how many of them there were, but they obeyed, coming closer and gathering round. It was like watching a weird prayer meeting where the priest, dressed in a cheap grey suit and scuffed black leather shoes, looked like a cop. Except for the eyes. With Rafael it was all about the eyes.

Rafael's audience, his congregation, didn't seem to care what he looked like, their faces rapt as they stared at him. Gabe knew what was happening, that every one of them was listening to his silent instructions. Instructions he wasn't being allowed to hear. Then Rafael pointed at the chapel and, like soldiers on parade, everyone turned in unison and did as they'd been told. Whatever that had been.

Rafael spun round and faced Gabe, holding out the shovel. "Here, boy," he said. "Dig."

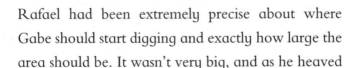

Rafael had been extremely precise about where Gabe should start digging and exactly how large the area should be. It wasn't very big, and as he heaved earth out of the two metre by one metre wide hole it was clear that this was not to be his final resting place. He hoped what had been buried here wasn't down too deep as the ground was hard and he could already feel a couple of blisters coming up on his hands.

"Keep going, boy," Rafael hissed, bending down to whisper in his ear. "You have an eternity of rest awaiting you."

At about the one-metre level there was a dull thud as the shovel hit something hollow; a few minutes later Gabe cleared the earth away to reveal the flat wooden lid of a metal-bound chest. It was about forty-five centimetres long and some twenty-five centimetres wide, the wood and the metal blackened with age.

"At last…"

Gabe looked up and saw the expression on Rafael's face. He was ecstatic, almost close to tears. Which most likely meant, he thought, that they had to be on the final stretch. This was the end of the road, for him anyway, and he had a real bad feeling in the pit of his stomach that whatever was in this box was only going to make Rafael even more powerful.

"Get it out, set it free!"

Gabe dug round the edges of the chest until he found the handles at either end. Reaching down he tried to pull on them, but the metal had corroded so badly over the centuries they both broke off in his hand.

"Clear more earth, boy. Use the shovel as a lever!"

Gabe wanted to yell at the man to damn well use it as a lever himself, but the words never made it out of his mouth and all he could do was silently curse as he slid the shovel blade down the gap at one end of the chest and pulled back on the handle. There was a tiny shift, then a small bit more and finally the ancient strongbox was free. Rafael hurriedly knelt down opposite Gabe and between the two of them they heaved the chest up and out on to the ground.

"So long… It has been *so* long." Rafael gently brushed away soil caked on to the rusted metal decoration surrounding the keyhole. "But we are together once again…"

Gabe watched Rafael use a small stick to clean earth out of the lock, then stand up and look over his shoulder at the chapel. "Pick it up," he said, pointing at the chest. "They are ready, take it in."

Inside the chapel candles and incense had been lit, the air heavy with anticipation. The place was packed tight, with the men and women crowded together into a heaving mass leaving only a narrow gap just wide enough for Gabe to make his way through them to the back, straining under the weight of the old strongbox. The box smelled dank and musty, its surface clammy with the heavy odours soaked up by the wood during the ages it had spent underground since Rafael had originally buried it.

And now he had it back.

There was a sharp intake of breath as Gabe stepped into the makeshift aisle the congregation had created, and all eyes were on him, glinting in the wavering candlelight. Almost as one, the crowd started to whisper and shuffle, the noise rising and falling in soft, chittering waves of sound that echoed dully off the chapel walls.

Gabe wondered what had happened to Father Simon's body, and the owl's feathers and carcass, as there was no sign of them. At the back of the chapel, against the rear wall, he could now see the altar, surrounded by candles; there was no sign of the dog Rafael had killed and ripped the heart out of, either.

The dream image of the ritual slaughters he'd witnessed flashed in his head again and Gabe tried to step back, but Rafael shoved him and he stumbled forward. The people on either side caught him, holding him upright, and pushed him on. Multitudes of fingers feeding him towards the altar like he was in the gut of a beast. Like he was being digested.

"Put it on the ground, boy."

Gabe's body obeyed the instruction, then stood back up. There was a swell of voices around him, murmurs rustling like cold, dead leaves, as Rafael knelt down in front of the chest. He reached into his jacket pocket and brought out a key, which he carefully inserted in the lock.

The noise in the old chapel started to build.

Rafael slowly turned the key, and Gabe saw that he was now wearing the gold rings and bracelets.

The people were becoming agitated, moaning now and crowding forward.

Rafael lifted the lid and yellow candlelight reflected off what was inside, making it glow like embers.

Rafael reached into the chest, picked up the object and held it above his head.

A cry went up, a mixture of joy and pain that turned to a roar when Rafael stood to face the crowd and placed the gold skull mask topped with snakes and feathers on his head. Gabe was stunned. Right here in front of him, his terrible dreams were being made real.

Two of the congregation stepped forward, bent down and together brought something else out of the chest. They pulled it up, centuries of dust billowing out from the still-colourful fabric as it unfolded, floating lazily in the air. Reverently they placed the floor-length cloak over Rafael's shoulders.

The crowd bellowed and Rafael raised his head to look at the roof.

"It is the time!"

Gabe saw the skull had a hinged jaw that moved when the wearer spoke, which somehow made this scene even eerier. Dead man speaking.

"Get him!"

Get him? Gabe braced himself, thinking he was about to be grabbed and dragged to the altar. He tried not to let the pictures flash in front of him, wanted more than anything not to remember the other boys he'd witnessed being sacrificed. Tried and failed to forget what he knew was going to happen next.

But nothing happened.

He stayed where Rafael had left him, unable to move or even turn his head a little to see what was causing the disturbance he could hear. Those of the crowd that he could see were expectantly peering behind them towards the entrance to the chapel, and he could hear the scuffling and muffled grunting noises getting nearer. And then four men appeared, carrying between them a desperate boy, writhing, thrashing and kicking. It was the same as in his dreams, each man was holding a limb, so their unfortunate victim looked like he'd been caught, twisting, mid star jump. This was the person who was going to be sacrificed to whatever depraved gods Rafael worshipped, not him. Not yet, anyway.

Gabe forced himself to look at the boy's face; the only thing which stopped him collapsing to the ground when he did was that he couldn't move.

It was Anton.

Gabe felt tears well up in his eyes and fall unchecked down his cheeks. The shock of seeing his best friend here, being taken like an animal to the slaughter, took the breath out of him. He was going to have to stand, helpless and pathetic, and watch Anton die in the worst possible way.

"You will not watch, boy." Rafael appeared right in front of Gabe, blocking his view of the altar.

Gabe stared at him, unable to think straight, not really hearing a word he was saying. All he could think about was Ant... What was he doing here? How had these crazed people caught him? Was it somehow *his* fault? Had Rafael chosen Ant because he was Gabe's friend?

"He put himself in our hands, offered himself to us, in a way, by trying to help you." Rafael slid a hand out from inside his cloak. "And now it is *your* turn to offer *us* something... To repay the debt you owe to *me* for your ingratitude."

Gabe felt something being pressed into his chest and his hands automatically moved to hold it.

"Take this." Rafael stepped back. "Handle it with care, treat it with the respect an instrument of the gods deserves."

Gabe looked down and saw he was holding the gold knife, its wide, curved blade shining like a vicious grin. For a moment he thought he must be imagining what was happening. And then he looked up and saw Rafael, smiling at him, move to his right and bow slightly, like he was welcoming him somewhere. As he stood aside he revealed the altar and Gabe saw Anton, pinioned like a butterfly, his T-shirt ripped apart to expose his chest. He was being held down by the four men. A fifth person, a woman, had a rope around his neck, so all Anton could do was stare at the ceiling of the chapel.

"You have seen this, you know what must be done," Rafael whispered in Gabe's ear. "So, do it…"

Gabe's hands locked around the knife handle, and he found himself walking towards the altar, arms raised high above his head.

Chapter Forty-Four

Gabe could hear his heart thundering, feel the sweat joining his tears as it poured down his face, the salt making his eyes sting. Inside he was screaming to himself that in any other reality he would be spinning round and lashing out at Rafael, splitting *his* ribcage open with the knife blade, reaching in and pulling out *his* beating heart. Not about to do it to Anton.

He was being used to kill his own friend, who hadn't known the danger he was getting himself into – how could Ant have known that he would be risking everything by trying to help? Of all the grim and appalling things Rafael had ever done, in all the times he had been alive, this had to be the worst. There was no reason to it… How could a person be *so* twisted? How could Rafael be making him do this? Yet here he was, about to make a sacrifice of someone he'd grown up with, known since he was four years old!

Behind him Gabe was aware of the assembled company of Rafael's followers standing in silence, a hushed, eager quiet hanging in the air like a hawk waiting to fall on its prey.

"They await," Rafael said quietly, inside Gabe's head. "They have been waiting for *so* long, boy, and now is their time… It is now the Next Time, and you have the honour of spilling the first blood, the first of *so* much blood! Everything is ready, a sickle moon hangs over us and nothing can stop this great day from dawning! Do it *now*!"

The hideous thing was that Gabe could feel his mouth twisting into a ghastly impression of a grin… Rafael was making him smile as he looked straight down into Anton's panic-stricken eyes, bloodshot from crying, wide with abject fear and full of disbelief. The last thing Ant was going to see would be the person he trusted most smirking as he was about to kill him.

Gabe fought against the pull of his muscles, trying to override Rafael's instructions, but it was no use. Then, as his arms pistoned down, he made one final, violent effort to alter the course of the knife. It coincided with Anton's last-ditch attempt to escape, surprising his captors by jerking sideways like he'd been hit with a thousand bolts of lightning. The two events were only milliseconds apart, but that was all it needed for the knife to miss its target. Instead of crashing through Anton's sternum and splitting it apart, the razor-sharp blade merely glanced off the lower side of his ribcage and landed with the full force of Gabe's downward thrust on the stone altar slab.

The crowd still saw blood and roared its approval. They thought the job had been done. Next they expected to see the final cut and they were all holding their breath for the long-awaited sight of a still-beating heart held up high. It had been promised to them.

Gabe turned and found himself looking straight at Rafael. Direct eye contact. Locked on, like a laser-guided missile. And then the strangest thing happened. Behind the gold mask Rafael blinked first.

For a moment, a precious few seconds, as Rafael tried to take in the wholly unacceptable truth that events had not gone as he had planned, his hold over Gabe momentarily slipped. The survival circuit in

Gabe's brain sensed this and kicked into action. It was involuntary, his spirit's last desperate attempt to cling to life. The deep, feral urge to exist took over and Gabe swung round like a crazed dervish, the knife held out horizontally at neck height.

It sliced open the jugular of the man holding one of Anton's arms, a massive gout of arterial blood pumping out and spraying across the chapel.

It caught Rafael's left arm at the elbow as he unthinkingly tried to defend himself, severing the joint completely.

And as Gabe spun full circle, the blade's journey ended as it embedded itself deep in the head of the man still holding one of Anton's legs.

Harrowing screams filled the air, as the herd instinct Rafael had created to control the congregation dissolved into a mindless panic. Trapped in this small, cave-like space, ancient fears bubbled up to the surface, made all the worse when first one person, then two more, got pushed too close to a cluster of candles and their clothes caught fire.

In the middle of the spiralling mayhem Gabe saw Anton, still lying on the altar even though no one was holding him down any more.

"*Ant!*"

Scared witless, holding the bloody rags of his T-shirt against his wound, Anton shrank back.

"We gotta get outta here, guy." Gabe glanced over his shoulder at the hellish chaos behind him. "We *gotta* go!"

"You … you…" Anton shook his head as he pointed an accusing finger at Gabe.

"No, no! That wasn't me, Ant, it wasn't!"

"It *was* you, boy!"

In the growing pandemonium, Gabe had forgotten about Rafael. Bad move. He looked round to see the man weaving unsteadily behind him, the gold skull mask shimmering as it reflected the flames that now licked at the wooden rafters of the chapel roof.

"*You* did this!" screeched Rafael, and seemingly oblivious of what had happened to him, he swung what was left of his arm out, blood flying. "All my plans, so carefully laid… All gone, because of *you*, boy!"

Behind Rafael, Gabe could see a screaming, hysterical mass of people, more and more with their clothes and hair ablaze, all crammed together as they fought manically to get out. Except for some reason the doors were refusing to open. If there was ever a vision of Hell, he thought, this was it. And he and Anton were trapped in it too.

"I promised you would die!" Rafael yelled above the din, bending down to yank the sacrificial knife out of his dead follower's head. "And you will... Both of you will! Rafael Delacruz has *always* been a man of his word!"

As Rafael raised the knife a small, overweight man, ablaze from head to toe like a vast tallow lamp, staggered by, screaming hysterically. What happened next wasn't something he'd had time to think through, it was an unconscious, reflex action, pure and simple. Gabe kicked out wildly at the burning man, who reeled sideways, arms flailing, into Rafael. The ancient fabric of his cloak, tinder-dry, caught fire instantly, going up with an audible *whoomp* and enveloping Rafael in a deadly cocoon of flames. Gabe reeled back from the heat, mesmerized by the roaring inferno in front of him. Rafael was gold all over now.

Unable to drag his eyes away, Gabe couldn't believe it when he saw the man, his flesh now melting to the bone, pull his shoulders back. Knife raised, he was ignoring reality and somehow going on the attack again.

Which could not be happening because *he was on fire...* But instead of killing Rafael, the flames seemed to be feeding him, giving him even greater power. Then Rafael's chest rose, as if he was about to hold his breath, and it looked like the fire was being drawn deep inside him, making it appear that his heart was glowing a fierce orange.

The attack never came. Instead, quite suddenly, Rafael collapsed on to the chapel floor, the flames dying with the man. Gabe stared at the lifeless body, not quite able to take in what had happened... The man who had promised to kill him was dead.

"What the hell is going on?"

Gabe looked back at Anton, who was watching him cautiously. "I'll tell you when we get out of here."

"And how exactly are we gonna do that, bro?" Anton slid awkwardly off the altar as burning debris began falling from the roof.

"Guess we could try busting a window, right?"

"Guess we could," Anton said, staying just out of reach of Gabe.

"I told you, it wasn't *me* doing that thing with the knife, Anton. Honest to god…"

"Sure *looked* a whole lot like you, dude." Anton shook his head. "We are toast, man… I mean, *literally*, we are toast if we don't shift our asses."

The only thing Gabe could see that he might be able to break a window with was the old strongbox. Bending down to pick up the chest, he stopped. "You hear that?"

Ant frowned. "What?"

"Sirens?"

"Could be… Let's not wait and see, man. Right?"

"Yeah, right…" Gabe picked up the chest, lighter now that the solid gold mask had been taken out, ran towards the nearest window and threw it…

Chapter Forty-Five

Gabe scrambled to his feet coughing, helped up by Anton who he'd insisted got out first. He looked back in through the busted window at the inferno – a complete nightmare scene he'd probably made worse by letting more air in – and knew they had just made it out before it was too late. He couldn't stop staring, stop feeling he should at least have tried to get someone else out.

"Them or us, man." Anton pulled him back. "It is what it is. There's nothing you coulda done."

In the distance the sirens were getting closer.

"What were you—?"

Anton and Gabe both started talking at once, Anton nodding for Gabe to go first.

"How did you, you know, get caught up in all this, Ant?" Gabe could smell burning and saw all the hair on his forearms had been singed off. "I had a fit when I saw you being dragged in."

Anton moved further away from the chapel, wincing slightly and holding his side as he walked. "See, it was all over everywhere, that you'd got yourself arrested? So I went down to that house near the church." Anton looked at the blood on his hand and absentmindedly wiped it off on his jeans. "Saw you roll up with this guy, you acting like you were all kinda spaced out, and wondered what was up... It was weird, like I was sure there were *gun*shots from inside the house? But the cops outside ignored it, and then you come walking back out like nothing's up. Like I said, weird. So I followed you."

"You did?"

"Sure." Anton glanced at the approaching squad cars, lights going, sirens adding to the wailing from inside the chapel. "Like, at first I just wanted to see you were OK, which you were. And second, I thought the guy was a cop. Then I figured maybe he wasn't a *good* cop, when he drove out to this place."

"Why didn't you call someone, your cell out of juice?"

"I *did* call someone, I'm not a total knucklehead. It just wasn't 911." Gabe frowned. "I thought it would take too long to get them to take me seriously, OK? Thought I should stay following you."

"So who…"

"I got Stella's number from one of the other girls and called her, told her everything. Figured she could sell it better'n me. Time it's taken them to get here, looks like she had trouble too."

"But how'd they get you, Ant, what happened?"

"I dunno… Saw a coyote outside this place, like it was on guard? I figure it must've got my scent or something, cos the next thing I know it's coming for me and has me cornered, and then these couple of spooky guys appear and take me off." Anton flopped back against a gravestone, grimy and blood-spattered and looking like a refugee from a war zone. "OK, bro, your turn. You were stupid enough to have *some*thing to do with Benny Gueterro and ended up here? How did that happen?"

"This place –" Gabe nodded towards the chapel – "it's nothing to do with Benny."

"He's dead, and his van was outside that house, right? There's a connection, dude."

"Yeah, kinda…" Gabe looked past Anton at the

squad cars now screeching to a halt, uniformed men bursting out of them. "But you're gonna have to wait for me to explain what it is."

Gabe sat on the red moulded plastic seat, Anton next to him. They were in a room, in some department, in a hospital, somewhere. Neither of them had asked where they were, or what time it was, both of them were strung out and exhausted. It had been the strangest of days.

They'd been through the ER, they were clean, checked out and patched up. Anton had needed patching up more than Gabe, who just had a few burns and a couple of blisters as physical evidence of what he'd been through. The plasters on Gabe's hands were no match for the plate-size dressing Anton had over the gash on his side, for which he'd been given a tetanus jab and a couple of serious painkillers. They'd been brought into the room by a nurse, who'd given them some candy bars and cans of soda and told them their parents should be arriving soon. Oh, and by the way, there were some officers who wanted to talk to them too.

Gabe opened a candy bar and took a bite. "Is there a story we have to get straight?"

"You tell me, bro," Anton popped a can. "It's your gig, all I did was follow."

This was the first time they'd been on their own since the police had arrived at the chapel and up till then they'd had no chance to talk. Now there was time, Gabe didn't know what to think or say. Maybe he should just claim he was suffering from amnesia. It might work. Just deny all knowledge, of anything, and keep denying it no matter what they said. He sighed and stuffed the rest of the bar in his mouth. That plan might've worked, except that Anton and Stella were involved. Back to square one.

"If you tell the truth, you don't have to remember anything." Anton chugged some soda. "I read that somewhere."

"You, read?"

"Sure, why not? You think I'm stupid?"

"No, I just never seen you with a book. Who said that, anyway ... the remembering thing?"

"No idea. Sounds reasonable, though, right?"

Gabe sat back in the chair and stared at nothing in particular, thinking, yeah, it did sound reasonable.

But only if the truth wasn't going to make you sound like you were completely insane. Which to be be honest, with himself at least, he was somewhat surprised he wasn't, considering what he'd been through these last few days.

"I also read it was better to make no excuses than make bad ones."

Gabe turned and stared at his friend like he was a total stranger who had just dropped in out of nowhere.

Anton finished his can. "Just saying, bro."

"Are you a replicant or something?"

The door opened before Anton could reply. A man in a beige suit came in; he left the door ajar.

"My name's Mr de Soto, Detective de Soto. Your parents are here, but we need to have a word with you both before you go home." The detective jerked a thumb out of the room. "Just down the corridor…"

Chapter Forty-Six

After retrieving her car from outside Father Simon's place, Stella and Gabe had driven Anton over so he could pick up the scooter. She'd pulled over and parked near to where Anton had left it, but so far they'd all just stayed in the car, Anton in the back, silently watching the Vespa. Which was a weird thing for them all to be doing for a number of reasons, including that it was a Tuesday, late morning, but they weren't bunking off school. They were 'recuperating from their recent traumatic experiences', as some news report had put it.

If you believed everything you heard on the TV news what they were recuperating from had been a drugs-related thing, which centred on Benny Gueterro, and seemed to be a mash-up of Stella's and Gabe's stories. As Anton said, these days it was getting harder and harder to tell the difference between fiction, news and reality TV.

The one recurring element in every version of events had was the rogue-cop angle, and for some reason this had taken a lot of the heat off their part in what had gone down. Apparently rogue cops were the kind of meaty story journalists seemed to like – a lot. But what really made them disappear pretty much completely off the radar was the fact that on Monday – a scant twenty-four hours after a priest disappeared, a drug dealer got murdered outside the priest's house and an as yet unspecified number of people died in a fire at a historic chapel – a *major* political scandal erupted in Washington.

And it turned out that every single part of the media liked those stories best of all. Especially as this scandal looked like it might have the potential not only to go all the way to the front door of the White House, but right inside the Oval Office as well. Christmas had come early to newsrooms across the country and everything else got wiped off the agenda. Who cared about local news when there was some serious dirty laundry being washed in public? Exactly nobody. Even their parents were cutting them fairly major amounts of slack, for the moment.

"Are we gonna get away with it?" Anton blew and popped some bubblegum.

"Get away with what?" Gabe looked over his shoulder.

"Whatever it is that we did…" Another bubble popped. "Or *you* guys did and *I* got mixed up in and had my ribs shaved. Did you say sorry yet, dude?"

"A million times already."

"Not nearly enough…" Anton stuck a leg up between the seats, rested his trainer next to Gabe's head and tapped it with the toe. "So, look, not only do I feel like a third wheel here, guys … but you, bro, you owe me an explanation."

Stella looked sideways at Gabe. "If you say anything you'll have to kill him…"

"I already nearly did that." Gabe swivelled round in his seat. "OK, I'll tell, simple as I can…"

"What? OK, first you think I don't read books, and *now* you have to give me the nursery-rhyme version?"

"Aw geez, Anton, gimme a chance, OK? Please?" Gabe turned back and stared out of the windscreen, shaking his head. "This is all so damn crazy I don't even know if I believe it myself…"

Anton grinned. "Try me. I have a very active imagination, my kindergarten teacher said so."

Stella shot him a glance. "Give Gabe a break?"

Where did he start? Gabe shook his head and dived in. "You remember that storm a week, ten days ago? Well, I was up in the canyon and found something, a skeleton … and some gold. And I also kind of brought some old Spanish priest back to life…"

Ant listened, not interrupting for once, while Gabe told him everything. Finally, Gabe's throat tightened and he stopped talking, like he'd run out of words for a moment. The silence began to stretch like a wire pulled tight. Then Anton popped a big one.

"So, what happened to the gold?"

Gabe looked at Stella in disbelief, then back at Anton. "Really?"

"Really what, man?"

"That's *all* you want to know?"

Anton shrugged. "Follow the money, right?"

"It all got…"

People always said traumatic events got burned into your memory, and Gabe had a feeling he was never, ever going to be able to get rid of those final horrific moments in the chapel… The sight of Rafael, flames consuming his crumpled body. Gabe shivered involuntarily. He stared out of the car, his gaze finally coming to rest on a red hatchback. It was still there, where Rafael had parked it.

"It all got what, bro?"

Gabe looked away from the car and turned round. "It was, you know, all in the chapel, Ant. Rafael was wearing it…"

"Damn shame." Anton opened a door and began to get out, then leant between the seats to check the dashboard. "It's kinda lunchtime … and there's fresh home-made lasagne at mine. Want to meet me there, or you two got plans?"

"Lasagne sounds good." Gabe turned to Stella. "Right?"

"Sounds good."

"OK." Anton got out and shut the door. "See ya there…"

Another silence stretched out, with no one around this time to pop a bubble and break it. Finally, Stella turned the ignition and started the Toyota.

"Gabe?"

"Yeah?"

"Why d'you think you never got taken over by Rafael, like the others?"

"He said…" Gabe closed his eyes and looked upwards, his voice hushed. "He said he recognized me, that I'd been with him before and was supposed to be with him, some kind of disciple…"

"That's not true." Stella indicated and waited for a gap in the traffic.

"But what if it is?"

"It just isn't, OK?" Stella edged out. "But the gold… It did get burned up in the fire, didn't it?"

Gabe nodded slowly, wondering why she was asking. "Yeah, it did. All of it, Stella. Truthfully… All of it… I saw it happen."

"What're you gonna do with the money?"

Gabe's head began to fill with all kinds of thoughts… That he had over two thousand dollars hidden at home… That he would find some way of doing some good with the money… That he needed, *badly* needed to sit down with his dad and talk… He would do that as soon as he got back…

"Gabe? Are you all right?"

Gabe slowly unclenched his fists. "Yeah, really, I'm fine… I was just, you know, thinking…

Thinking that I'm done with thinking about that stuff. It was evil, I wish I'd never found it."

"It was an accident, you didn't go looking, right?"

"But Rafael said I'd found him, made it sound like I'd done it on purpose…" Gabe replied, remembering exactly how he'd felt when he touched the gold, when it was his. "And you can't find something if you weren't looking for it in the first place."

"Know what you've go to do? It's simple – you gotta believe."

"Believe what?"

"That Rafael was lying."

Gabe glanced at the red car as they drove past it and felt a coldness, like a knife being run down his spine.

He didn't notice the coyote, a grey silhouette amongst the shadows across the street.

Dare you collect the whole series?

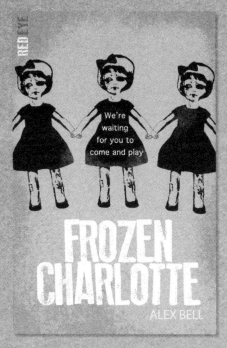

ISBN: 978-1-84715-453-8

EISBN: 978-1-84715-504-7

Frozen Charlotte

Alex Bell

Following the sudden death of her best friend, Sophie
hopes that spending the summer with family on a
remote Scottish island will be just what she needs. But
the old schoolhouse, with its tragic history, is anything
but an escape. History is about to repeat itself.
And Sophie is in terrible danger…

Also available as ebooks

The
nightmare
begins
when you're
awake

SLEEPLESS

LOU MORGAN

ISBN: 978-1-84715-455-2

EISBN: 978-1-84715-573-3

Sleepless

Lou Morgan

The pressure of exams leads Izzy and
her friends to take a new study drug they find online.
But one by one they succumb to hallucinations,
nightmares and psychosis. The only way to
survive is to stay awake…

ISBN: 978-1-84715-457-6

EISBN: 978-1-84715-645-7

Dark Room

Tom Becker

When Darla and her dad move to Saffron Hills, she
hopes it'll be a new start. But she stands no chance of
fitting in with the image-obsessed crowd at her new
school. Then one of her classmates is killed while taking
a photo of herself. When more teens die it appears that
a serial killer is on the loose – the 'Selfie Slayer'.
Can Darla unmask the killer before it's too late?

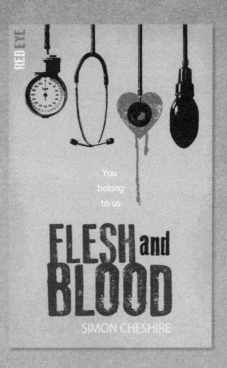

RED EYE

You
belong
to us

FLESH and BLOOD

SIMON CHESHIRE

ISBN: 978-1-84715-456-9

EISBN: 978-1-84715-574-0

Flesh and Blood

Simon Cheshire

When Sam hears screams coming from a
nearby house, he sets out to investigate. But the
secrets hidden behind the locked doors of Bierce
Priory are worse than he could ever have imagined.
Uncovering the horror is one thing, escaping is another.

An extract from
Flesh and Blood
by Simon Cheshire

It shook me like a slap in the face. It was some distance away, and heavily muffled by the double glazing, but it was so sharp, so filled with terror, that it cut into my mind like a razor blade. It was a howling shriek of pain.

I flinched, and my eyes popped open. I blinked and squinted in the sudden rush of light from my lamp. Fumbling, I switched it off.

What the hell was that?

I lay absolutely still. There was silence, not even the occasional ticking of the heating.

Lying there, in the calm and the darkness, I wondered if I could have dreamed it. Surely, a sound like that...? Was it one of those vivid dreams you have to consciously shrug off, one of those nightmare impressions that leaves you doubting that you're back in reality when you wake up? I wanted it to be a dream. After all, a scream in the dead of night was...

My sleep-fogged mind circled groggily around the idea of getting up to investigate. I twisted around on the mattress and looked over at the dim glow of my alarm clock. I'd put it over by the door, so that I couldn't roll over and switch it off in the mornings.

2:12 a.m. My heart was thumping. How long I lay there for, I don't know. Several minutes, at a guess. Not a single sound came from outside. With every passing moment, the urge to fling my duvet aside and rush to the window grew stronger. But, at the same time, the continuing silence fuelled my doubts.

Instinct told me that the scream was real. It had knocked me out of sleep. The only time such a thing had ever happened to me before was when a car windscreen had been broken down in the street below my bedroom, years ago. On the other hand, plain common sense said it was nothing but my own imagination.

What if...

Another murder? Like the body by the river? No, we were too far from the territory of any gangs for that to be the explanation. Elton Gardens was almost half a mile down the hill. The scream had been distant, a lot further away than the Giffords' house, or the Daltons', but it had still woken me. It had been distinct. It couldn't have come from anywhere near the river. It could only have come from the Priory.

I couldn't let it go. I couldn't hear something like that and not act. Someone had screamed for their life, someone...

...female. That was a female voice.

Emma! What if Emma was in danger?

I rubbed the last of the sleep from my eyes and quickly clambered to my feet. The room wasn't cold, but still a shock after the warmth of my bed. I rushed over to the window and peered out nervously. There was a very faint glint of light visible from the street lamps on Maybrick Road, largely obscured by the trees on the Priory's land. For the first time, it struck me that there was no street lighting in Priory Mews, none at all.

Call the police? More indecision clawed at me.

No, if it *was* Emma who was in trouble, then even a slight delay could have terrible consequences. I had to act now! Fumbling in haste, I wrapped myself in my dressing gown and pulled on yesterday's socks.

I turned and hurried down to Mum and Dad's room. The door was slightly ajar. A brief glimpse inside told me that they hadn't heard anything. They were dead to the world.

I said I would write this account as objectively as I could. That's what a responsible journalist would do. So, in the interests of objectivity, I must record, here and now, that the decision to leave my room that night was a profound mistake.

If only I'd woken my parents, if only I'd listened to the silence and my own doubts, if only I hadn't been in such a rush to do something heroic, then everything would have turned out differently. Leaving the house that night was the spark that lit the fuse. My suspicions would still have been aroused. I would still have asked questions, and investigated, and tried to find out where that scream had come from, but events would have unfolded in a very different way, and perhaps the worst of them might have been avoided.

The awful fact is, I wasn't thinking straight. It may be that I was still half asleep, I don't know. For whatever reason, it never even occurred to me that if it was indeed Emma who was in trouble, she had a household of adults around her to help. That one simple, obvious thought would have kept me in my room. I would have been very concerned, certainly, sleepless and even scared, but I wouldn't have been running for the front door.

However, the thought never entered my head. So that's that.

I ran downstairs, jammed on my school shoes and put my coat on over my dressing gown.

Cold night air pinched at me as I stepped outside. Priory Mews was as motionless as the corpse in the park. There was no far-off rumble of traffic. No stars were visible in the sky, the clouds were hanging as low and thick as they had the previous day.

I stood a few metres from my front door, watching, listening. I hugged my arms in tightly, but couldn't stop shivering. I tried to breathe as quietly as I could, straining my ears to pick up something, anything that might give me a clue about what to do now. My breath clouded around my face.

Gradually, my eyes were becoming accustomed to the dark. The outlines of my house, and of the Giffords' and the Daltons', were slowly filled in with grey-on-grey details. I could see the road surface beneath my shoes.

Our neighbours' homes were in complete darkness. Their sleep hadn't been broken either.

Taking delicate steps, I walked around to the side of our house, on to the grassy area beside our garden gate, heading for the Priory. I had to move slowly, even on the grass, because I still wasn't sure of the exact layout.

The large rear garden of Bierce Priory was surrounded by a very tall, black wrought-iron fence. At the side, a narrow padlocked gate led on to the steep hill overlooking the park, and the path down to the river.

I stepped stealthily along by the railings. They were too closely placed for anyone to squeeze through, and too high to climb without help.

I stood motionless again, shivering a little less as I acclimatized to the chill of the night. From there,

I could just about make out the Priory's looming shape. It rose up into the sky like jagged teeth.

I watched and waited but heard nothing, saw nothing. I began to doubt myself again. Perhaps there was nothing to hear other than the sped-up beating of my own heart, and the throb of blood through my ears. Then … I did hear something.

A gasping sound. A sort of agonized panting. And a slight rustling, like feet tramping slowly through long grass.

I felt as if my heart would stop. I reached out and gripped the freezing cold-railings with both hands. The sounds were definitely coming from the grounds of the Priory. Somewhere over to the left. They seemed to be moving away from the building. Towards me.

I screwed up my face, willing my eyes to pick out something I could identify. The gasping sound was getting closer. It seemed almost like sobbing now, like pain and terror crushed down into exhaustion.

Movement!

I caught sight of a shape. Low, close to the ground, moving slowly towards the fence.

The nightmare begins when you're awake

SLEEPLESS
LOU MORGAN

ISBN: 978-1-84715-455-2

Are you ready for your close-up?

DARK ROOM
TOM BECKER

ISBN: 978-1-84715-457-6

Some things are best left buried.

BAD BONES
GRAHAM MARKS

ISBN: 978-1-84715-454-5

You belong to us

FLESH and BLOOD
SIMON CHESHIRE

ISBN: 978-1-84715-456-9

She's coming for you

THE HAUNTING
ALEX BELL

ISBN: 978-1-84715-458-3

The forest will not forgive

FIR
SHARON GOSLING

ISBN: 978-1-84715-823-9

I know you're in there

CHARLOTTE SAYS
ALEX BELL

ISBN: 978-1-84715-840-6

"So creepy and amazing ... I loved it."
Zoella

We're waiting for you to come and play

FROZEN CHARLOTTE
ALEX BELL

ISBN: 978-1-84715-453-8

Hunt or be hunted

SAVAGE ISLAND
BRYONY PEARCE

ISBN: 978-1-84715-827-7

They're watching They're waiting

WHITEOU
GABRIEL DYL

ISBN: 978-1-78895-072

REDEYE
Do you dare?